OVER ON THE
LONESOME SIDE

OVER ON THE LONESOME SIDE

James A. Ritchie

Walker and Company
New York

First published in the United States of America in 1991 by Walker Publishing Company, Inc.

Published simultaneously in Canada by Thomas Allen & Son Canada, Limited, Markham, Ontario

Library of Congress Cataloging-in-Publication Data
Ritchie, James A.
Over on the lonesome side / James A. Ritchie.
p. cm.
ISBN 0-8027-4118-5
I. Title.
PS3568.I814O94 1991
813'.54—dc20   91-3699
CIP

Printed in the United States of America

2 4 6 8 10 9 7 5 3 1

To my wife, Marla, whose love and patience are greater than any man deserves.

And to my niece, Mary Kay, who inspired the role model for the lead female character in this novel.

I owe you both more than I can ever repay.

CHAPTER 1

I WAS just easing down for a good night's sleep in the first real bed I'd seen in more than two months when the letter finally caught up with me. Judging by the envelope, it must have wound through half of Texas before finding me in El Paso, but at least it had reached me.

It was from an old friend up Alamitos way: a man I'd not seen in more than five years, but a man who'd given me a hand at a time when I needed it most. Now he needed help and was calling on me to give it. I cast a longing look at the bed and sighed. An hour later I was astride my horse and riding north out of Texas.

Come morning, I stopped in Las Cruces to eat and put up a few supplies, including an extra canteen, then pushed on into the Jornada del Muerto. It was already the fall of the year, but that desert felt like the hot side of hell. Cap, my big Appaloosa, had seen desert before and took the heat and choking dust better than I did.

We rode in an oven of shimmering heat waves under a sun that was molten gold and a sky like an endless sheet of brass. In all that long ride I saw no living thing except buzzards, jackrabbits, and a couple of lazy rattlesnakes looking for a bit of shade. And then we came through the desert and the country grew higher, greener and cooler.

Noon of the eighth day found me only five miles outside Alamitos. I was bone-tired, my hair matted, and my clothing stiff with dust. My head was filled with thoughts of a hot meal and a hotter bath, topped by a cold beer. It was then I came over the rise and saw the wagon.

It was sitting in the middle of the road, maybe a hundred

1

yards ahead, and five people milled around it. I stopped short, not wanting to ride into trouble before I knew what was what.

One of the five people looked to be an old man, another a young woman. Three horses were ground-reined twenty yards from the wagon, and it didn't take long to figure the riders of those horses were giving the old man and the girl a hard time.

Even as I watched, one of the men tied a rope around the spokes on a rear wheel of the wagon. A second man brought his horse over, looped the free end of the rope around his saddlehorn and put the spurs to his horse. Spokes cracked, splintered, and the wheel collapsed.

Now, my pa didn't raise any foolish children. Whatever was happening down there was none of my business, and all I'd likely get from sticking my nose into it would be a busted nose. It came to me that I should turn my horse and ride around the whole affair. Just this one time I was going to be sensible and mind my own business.

Then it happened. The old man grabbed one of the busted spokes and took a swing at the nearest man. He missed, and the man knocked him down. The old man hit square on his shoulder blades and I winced in sympathy. As the girl knelt beside him the tough shoved her over with his boot.

I swore under my breath and started Cap forward. I didn't go charging in like some damn-fool tenderfoot, but went ahead at a walk, the dusty, soft ground of the road muffling any sound Cap might have made.

Like most folks, I had a Colt .45 on my hip, and I carried a Winchester in a saddle scabbard, but I also had a Colt revolving shotgun hanging from the saddle by a rawhide thong. I took the shotgun loose, holding it close against my leg so it wouldn't be visible until I was up close. That shotgun held four rounds, each loaded with buckshot, and it might be enough to stop trouble before it started.

Something I noticed early on . . . not many men are foolish enough to argue with a shotgun at close range.

At thirty yards they still hadn't seen me. The girl tried to get up and was shoved down again, all three men now standing around her. I was close enough to hear the men laughing and the girl spittin' fire, telling all three of them where to get off. And then one of the men began to unbutton his pants.

Fool thing, that. You could steal, and folks might write it off as sowing wild oats. You could kill a man, and the law, what little there was of it, would like as not look the other way. But women were scarce and valued accordingly. Touch a woman, and even most of the outlaws would lend a hand in stringing you from the nearest tree.

That Appaloosa of mine cat-footed another ten yards before one of the men looked up and saw us. He jumped about three feet straight up and yelled, *"Dancer."*

The man unbuttoning his pants turned, saw me, and his eyes opened wide. You never saw a man button up his pants so fast in your life. He got the last button in the hole and the three of them lined up, hands near guns, and watched me come. At fifteen feet I stopped, keeping my horse turned so the shotgun stayed out of sight.

The shock of having me ride up wore off quick, and the big man, the one called Dancer, took a step toward me. He would go well over two hundred pounds, most of it in his arms and chest. His nose had been broken more than once, and a deep scar ran up his cheek and near one eye. He looked to be a man who would perfer his fists, but he wore a Colt, tied down like maybe he knew how to use it.

I looked the other two over, giving only a quick glance to each, and dismissed them. They were hangers-on, followers—the kind you'd hire to rough up someone or to shoot them in the back. Neither looked to be a gunhand, but each would follow Dancer.

If there was trouble, it would come from Dancer. Handle him, and the other two would lose all desire to fight.

"You ought to know better than to sneak up on a man that way," Dancer said. "It's a quick way to die."

"Just riding to Alamitos," I said. "Guess you were too busy to hear me coming."

His eyes narrowed and he jerked a thumb down the road. "Alamitos is that way. If you push hard, you can make it in an hour."

I grinned, patted my horse on the neck. "Could be, but Cap here is tired. So am I, come to think of it.

"Yes, sir. I been in the saddle since before daybreak and my soft side is starting to ask questions. Thought maybe I'd stop hereabouts and have a cup of coffee. You know, give Cap a chance to rest and my underside a chance to breathe."

Dancer didn't know what to think. I could see him turning it over in his mind, trying to decide if I was being smart, or if I was simply too dense to understand what was going on. After a minute he spread his legs a bit and slipped the thong off his pistol.

"You're butting into business that doesn't concern you," he said. "It's a bad habit and one that'll get you killed."

"That is a fact," I said. "It's a habit I've tried to break time and again, but you know how it is." I eased the muzzle of the shotgun over the saddle, not pointing it at Dancer but laying it out where he could see it plain. He looked down the cavernous muzzle and licked his lips. "Thing about a habit like mine," I said, "is that it sometimes gets other men killed. I'd feel real bad if it happened again.

"The way I look at it, we both made the same mistake. You butted into these folks' business, now I've stuck my nose in yours. It's a shame when a country gets so crowded that a man can't have any privacy.

"Tell you what, suppose you boys ride out, I'll have my cup of coffee and we'll forget the whole thing?"

Dancer didn't like any of it and I knew he was wondering

whether or not he could take me. I could read it in his eyes and in the nervous way his hand twitched near the butt of his gun. I was young, but so was Billy the Kid who had a reputation in these parts and was credited with killing a dozen men at last count.

And a shotgun flat doesn't give a damn how old the finger is that pulls the trigger.

Dancer looked at me, the shotgun, then the girl. It was clear he wanted her in the worst kind of way, so he must have been going crazy trying to figure the odds. At last the tension drained from his shoulders. "All right," he said. "We'll call it a draw this time."

He started toward his horse and the other two followed. I sighed, swore quietly, knowing it wasn't over. Call it suspicion or instinct, but I knew Dancer was going to turn and draw. Maybe it was the way his shoulders stayed tight and ready, or the careful way he measured each step, but I *knew* it was coming.

I turned Cap a little to keep the shotgun in line, and waited. Dancer took two more steps, then pivoted on his heel, his hand sweeping down and coming back up full of gun. I've no doubt he thought himself a fast man with a pistol. Well, we all make mistakes from time to time.

This mistake cost Dancer his life. I waited until his pistol cleared leather, then tilted the shotgun and pulled the trigger.

The shotgun roared, bucked in my hands, and through the powder smoke I saw the load of buckshot slam into Dancer like a leaden fist. He went down as if poleaxed, and there was no need for anyone to count to ten. Those other two stood there looking at me, scarce breathing for fear I'd shoot again. One of them clutched a bloody streak along his neck where a stray buckshot had burned him.

"Throw him over the saddle and ride out," I said. "If I see either one of you again I'll shoot you on sight."

They did it, but the one with the bloody neck gave me a

hard look. "The boss ain't going to like this," he said. "Dancer was a favorite of his."

"No accounting for taste. Now ride out."

They went off down the road, and I watched until they were out of rifle range in case one of them took a notion. When they were gone I slipped out of the saddle and knelt next to the old man and the girl.

"Thanks, mister," the girl said. "I think that man was going to—to . . ."

"Yes, ma'am," I said. "I reckon he was."

The old man had a nasty bruise on his cheek, but he was alert and fussin' to get up. The girl tried to hold him down, but he shook free of her. "Doggone it, child," he said, "it'll take better men than those to keep me down. Just help me to my feet, will you?"

I stood up and took his arm. "Best thing for him," I said. "Nobody ever died from a sore cheek."

I pulled the old man to his feet and he wobbled a little, caught his balance. He bit a huge chunk from a plug of tobacco, worked it around his mouth, and spat a stream of brown juice a good ten feet.

"Thanks, son. I'll be fine now. Say, you sure pulled our biscuits out of the fire. I'm obliged." He extended a calloused hand and I shook it.

"Name's Zeb Spencer," he said, "and this is my grand-daughter, Mary Kay."

The girl smiled. She had thick, brown hair that shaded off to red. Sort of auburn, I guess. A smattering of freckles ran across her nose and cheeks, and her eyes were a green that made me think of cool grass and shady trees.

She was pretty—beautiful, even—but she had a light in her eyes that made me nervous. I tipped my hat quick-like and turned my attention back to Zeb.

"Who were those boys?" I asked. "They didn't seem the type to be having fun at your expense unless put up to it."

Zeb touched his bruised cheek, winced at the pain. "They

were dead serious. Trouble was, they came riding up smiling and friendly as relatives on payday. The only one I'd seen before was Dancer, and him only in passing.

"You're right about one thing, though—it's dollars to doughnuts they were paid. I can't prove it, but I'd bet my ranch it was Colby Ryan who did the paying, too."

Never heard of him," I said. "What's he got against you?"

"Never heard of him, huh? That would sure set Colby off, that would. He figgers to be pretty big around here.

"As for what he has against us—Colby owns most of the land as far as you can see in any direction you care to look, and he wants the rest of it real bad. There must be twelve or fifteen small ranches about, but two or three of us own enough water rights to give Ryan control of the whole shebang.

"You understand, son, this is mostly speculation. Ain't nobody ever pinned nothing on Ryan, and it doesn't look like they ever will. Of course, toughs and gunhands are a dime a dozen around this country now, and it might be Ryan had nothing to do with it.

"Speakin' of gunhands, you sure handled that shotgun mighty slick. Guess you've had trouble before today?"

I didn't smile. "A time or two."

If what Zeb thought about this Colby Ryan was true, and it was a common enough story, this whole territory could erupt in a full-scale range war at any moment. Damn near every range war I knew anything about was started by some rancher deciding he wanted one more acre.

Me, I'd been up against hard times before, and I knew how deadly it could get in a hurry if Ryan was land hungry. Normally it wouldn't be any of my business and I'd keep on riding until I was well clear of it. This time was different.

The letter calling for help tied me to the area as surely as any rope might, and if it involved land in any way, Colby Ryan was a man I'd need to know more about.

I'm not so smart as some, but Pa always told me to sit down

and think a thing through before charging into it. It was a
piece of advice that had saved my bacon more than once.
Thing is, I think better over a cup of coffee.

"You know, Zeb, I wasn't kidding Dancer about that coffee.
Don't suppose you have any tucked away in your wagon?"

That Mary Kay moved quicker than scat. "You two keep
talking," she said. "It won't take a minute to start a fire and
put some water on."

She worried me. Unless I was badly mistaken, it seemed
she'd taken a fancy to me, maybe thought of me as some
kind of White Knight riding to the rescue. I'd the sudden
urge to get back in the saddle and not get out again until I
was somewhere in California. If it hadn't been for that letter
in my pocket, I'd have done it, too.

Not that I didn't want a wife and a family . . . someday.
And Mary Kay was sure enough lovely. Pretty as a speckled
pony in a field full of wild flowers, in fact, but when a man
runs single long enough he gets trap-shy, no matter how
attractive the bait.

But the whole time I talked to Zeb I found my eyes turning
toward Mary Kay. It was a pleasure to watch her do something as simple as make coffee. She was graceful, not a wasted
move anywhere, and she was true to her word. In not much
over a minute she had a fire blazing and a pot of water
starting to boil.

I looked away from her somewhat reluctantly. She was the
best bait I'd ever seen, and if I didn't watch my step I'd find
myself hauling long steel on a short chain.

"Let's look at that wagon," I told Zeb. "Might be something
we can do to get you moving again."

We looked, but the busted wheel was beyond fixing. "They
did it up proper," I said. "You'll need a new wheel before
you can go anywhere."

"We've two of them under the tarp, but I don't know about
getting one on. Might be we could empty the wagon and jack
her up with a pole."

I dug under the tarp and pulled one of the good wheels to the ground while Zeb loosened the nut that held the busted wheel in place. I put my back against the wagon, bent my knees, and got a good grip on the underside with both hands.

"When it comes off the ground," I said, "you jerk that busted wheel off and get the good one in place . . . fast."

Zeb looked doubtful, but rolled the wheel into position. I took a deep breath and slowly straightened my legs. The muscles in my arms and shoulders screamed in protest, but the wagon came off the ground. Zeb quickly put the new wheel on and locked it down with the nut.

"You've a sight of power in you, son," Zeb said. "I didn't think any one man could have lifted that weight."

"I swung a double-jack in a hard-rock mine for over a year. Best way I know to put muscle on a body."

"After seeing this, I can't argue with you." He wiped grease from his hands with an old rag, then bit a fresh chaw from his plug of tobacco.

We talked about range conditions and the like for a few minutes and Zeb gave me a general lay of the land. Knowing how to get around would be a help if I had to move quickly. Zeb was just warming up to the subject when the smell of brewing coffee drifted to us and Mary Kay yelled, "It's ready if you want it."

Mary Kay had built the fire in the shade of a big old white pine, and we sat cross-legged around it. The shade and the cool breeze felt wonderful after the heat of the desert, and a good cup of coffee would be just the thing to top it off.

Funny thing about coffee—I drank it even while out in the desert. I met a Mexican along the trail one time who told me that eating or drinking hot things actually cools a man off.

It's a roundabout way of thinking, but when you turn it around a time or two and kind of look at it from the bottom up, it does make an odd sort of sense. The way he put it was that hot drink or spicy food fools the body into believing it's even hotter than it really is, and so the body works overtime at cooling things down.

I suspect that Mexican had his tongue firmly in his cheek the whole time, but whether he was right or not, I favored a cup of coffee no matter the temperature, and at least he'd given me an excuse for drinking it. At any rate, when Mary Kay handed me a cup, letting her hand linger on mine a second longer than was necessary, I took it gratefully.

"Gramps likes it strong," she said, "so that's how I made it."

It was strong . . . strong enough to float a bullet, but that's how I like it, too.

I leaned back and looked over the country as I sipped at the coffee. Folks who've never been to New Mexico think of it as desert, and to an extent it is, but that's mostly to the south. The northern half of New Mexico has mountains and forest. And even some of the areas that are bone-dry and hot as hell in the summer can be covered with drifting snow and shivering at thirty below in the winter.

I'd never been in this area before, but a man meets folks from everywhere working in the mines or riding herd, and if he's even halfway smart he listens to them talk and remembers whatever they say about new country. Piecing together tales I'd heard around campfires with the information Zeb had given me, I thought I knew pretty much where I was.

If I was right, that was Mount Taylor off to the north a bit, and that hint of red below it was likely the thirty-mile stretch of lava beds that resulted when she blew her top God only knew how long ago. A handful of miles to the west the Continental Divide turned streams toward the Pacific, and a long day's ride due east the Rio Grande surged southward to Texas.

It was a rugged country, all standing on end, and reminded me of the country I grew up around. On first glance, and maybe on second, you wouldn't think of it as cow country, but other than providing lumber, it wasn't good for much else. You might not be able to run as many cows per acre as in Montana or Wyoming, but you generally had a lot more acres to work with.

I sat there in the shade and did some thinking about my past and my future. About all I'd ever known was hard times and hard work, and through it all the only thing I ever wanted was a small ranch and enough breeding stock to give me a start.

That, and maybe a wife to come home to at the end of a long, hard day. And I wanted sons who would grow strong and tall and proud. I wanted sons who would take up where I left off, building a life and a country.

There seemed small chance I'd ever have it. Starting a ranch takes money, lots of it, though here and there I'd known men who built huge ranches with nothing more than a rope and a branding iron. Mavericking, it was called. You just rode out on the open range and slapped your brand on anything that wasn't already wearing one.

That was fine in Texas, where longhorns ran wild by the thousands at the end of the war, but in New Mexico a man caught branding cattle he didn't own might find himself taking a long drop at the end of a short rope. Rustling was a range-wide problem, and folks took a hard line at anything that hinted at it.

Mary Kay must have refilled my cup without my taking notice, 'cause the next sip I took, the cup was full again and I burned my tongue. I yelped and jerked the cup away, spilling more hot coffee on my lap. I yelped again and Mary Kay laughed. Served me right for daydreaming. "Go ahead and laugh," I said. "I guess I had it coming."

"I'm sorry, but you should have seen your face."

I laughed at myself then, picturing how I must have looked, and felt better than I had in months.

"It just came to me," Zeb said. "We don't even know your name, son."

"It's Jim," I said. "Jim Darnell."

"Pleased to meet you, Jim. None of my business, but what brings a young fellow like you to Alamitos? We've not much to offer."

After seeing Mary Kay I might've argued that point. "Got a letter from an old friend asking me to come down and lend a hand," I said. "Maybe you know him? Name of John Lysander."

Zeb's face lit up and he grinned from ear to ear. "Know him? I should smile, I do! Why, John and me trapped all over this country before they was half a dozen white men west of the Big Muddy.

"John has one of the best ranches in the territory. It almost borders the southern boundary of Ryan's main ranch, and all that separates it from my own ranch is the tip of the Malpais and a few miles of rough country.

"John's a good man, but he's up against it hard. He controls more water than even Ryan, and he also has a darned sight more than his share of trouble with rustlers. If you ask me—hold on! *Jim Darnell* . . . Say, you ain't the same Jim Darnell that John tells that tall tale about, are you?"

John never could keep his mouth shut. "I've had a story told about me here and there," I said, "and John knows at least one of them. But if I know John, I imagine he's stretched it more than a little in the tellin'."

"Mary Kay," Zeb said, "you recollect the story I'm thinking of. Seems John was trapping some high-up country in Colorado a few years back and got snowed in with a no-account drifter named Marble something-or-other.

"One day this kid comes riding in with his father, only the father has two broke legs and the kid is riding a horse he stole from a band of Indians. The kid also has several pounds of gold, regular jewelry stuff, and Marble wants it for himself.

"To make a long story short, Marble tries to take the gold and the kid discourages him by putting three bullets where they count the most.

"That's how John tells it, anyway," Zeb finished, "and after seeing the way you handled Dancer, I wouldn't want to say it wasn't fact."

"I'll admit that's pretty much what happened," I said, "but told that way it makes me sound awful mean."

"It's one of John's favorite stories," Zeb said. "Mary Kay likes it, too. Why, she makes him tell it about once a month."

Mary Kay blushed a pretty red that darted from freckle to freckle across her face. "You make me sound terrible. It's only that Uncle John tells it so well. I never knew it was *true*."

I felt a little red-faced myself and did a fast trot to change the subject. "Tell me about Alamitos, Zeb. All I know about it is the name, and I got that from John's letter."

"Not much to tell, really. Like most towns hereabouts, it was founded by the Spanish, and up till ten years ago maybe fifty Mexican families lived there and that was it. Then somebody discovered cows could grow fat in these hot summers and find food and shelter in the winter.

"That was all it took. Ranchers moved in, the railroad followed, and we haven't had a peaceful day since.

"Alamitos is a shipping point now, and the only one for near two hundred miles. A dozen or more drives come through each fall and the town has grown accordingly. I can't say all the growth is for the good.

"There's two saloons for every honest business—not that I mind a drink now and again—and half the population runs to gamblers, gunhands, prostitutes, and thieves.

"It's a fine country for ranching, or even for setting up shop in town if your stick floats that way, but a man takes his life in his hands if he carries a worn silver dollar in his pocket. Ryan helps keep peace north of the tracks, 'cause trouble there is bad for business. Wander south of the tracks on a Saturday night and it's even odds you'll be shot, stabbed, or mugged."

"How did Ryan get so big? It would take years and a wheelbarrow full of money to build a spread the size of his, and from what you've said it doesn't seem he's been around long enough."

"You noticed that, did you? Truth is, Ryan has been here less than five years, and if he had any money squirreled away when he arrived, it wasn't noticeable. Then the few cows he owned all started having four calves each, bulls included, if you get my drift. A stagecoach or two ran into holdups, and suddenly Ryan was well-off.

"Well, sir, it wasn't long before a couple of small ranchers come up missing, and each time Ryan produced a bill of sale for their land. That's about where we are now."

"What about the law? Isn't there something the sheriff can do about Ryan?"

"Huh? What sheriff? We have a town marshal, Dave Burack, but he takes little enough note of what goes on inside of town unless it happens to be north of the tracks. What happens outside of town he figures is none of his business.

"He's mean, Burack is, and he likes nothing better than a chance to use his gun. I'm not saying he's on Ryan's payroll, but it amounts to the same thing."

"Looks like I might be walking into a stacked deck. Where does Ryan spend most of his time?"

"If he's in town you can find him at the Silver Slipper Saloon or the Bon Ton Hotel, both of which he has an interest in. He plays a bit of high-stakes poker at the Silver Slipper, and he usually wins.

"If he isn't in town, then he'll likely be at his home ranch, but wherever you find him, go careful. Colby Ryan is mean as a snake in the blind, but say what you will, the man can *fight*.

"Ryan hails from back East somewheres, and I've the notion he fought in the ring. He's fast, strong, and has a jaw like a granite slab. I saw him near kill two troublemakers in the Silver Slipper a few months back. Never worked up a sweat and enjoyed every minute of it."

It was a little after noon and time to be going. From the

looks of the sky it wouldn't be long before a late-summer storm rolled in from the west, and I wanted to be in Alamitos before it hit, though I doubted it would roll in before late evening. We put out the fire and tidied the wagon a bit, then rode off toward town.

Zeb and Mary Kay turned off toward their ranch a couple of miles short of town, and I rode on alone.

I looked back once and saw that Mary Kay was still watching me. I waved a hand and turned away. What Alamitos held in store would likely be a-plenty to keep me busy even without a girl like that to think of . . . even if she was the prettiest thing I'd ever seen.

CHAPTER 2

THE main drag of Alamitos clearly showed the prosperity brought by the cattle industry. Most of the older buildings were gone, replaced by freshly painted false fronts of wood, although here and there an adobe structure remained. Two of the buildings, the Bon Ton Hotel and the Bank of Alamitos, were built of brick, something rare in this part of the country.

Riding in near the height of the day, Alamitos seemed a peaceful, quiet town . . . a gangling man in a pinstripe suit came out of the bank and crossed in front of me, hurriedly counting a fistful of money before entering Bent's Mercantile. Two old ladies stood window-shopping in front of a dress shop, lifting their noses high as a pretty woman dressed in red walked past them.

Quiet enough on the surface, but I'd been in cow towns before and knew it wouldn't last. I could feel the buzz and tension of a growing town straining to break free. Come nightfall the saloons and gambling houses south of the tracks would awaken, prostitutes would begin to walk the streets, and cowboys from ranches far and near would drift into town for a few hours of fun before staggering back to the bunkhouse at midnight.

By first light those same cowboys would be back in the saddle, heads pounding and stomachs queasy from too much cheap whiskey, wondering why in hell they hadn't stayed home, vowing to forsake whiskey and women forever. It was a vow that would last until the next opportunity to go into town came along.

Here and there a curious face showed in a window or

doorway, some timidly, others with boldness, but all with the knowledge that a stranger riding into town was something to be wary of until his intentions were known. He might be nothing more than a drifting cowboy looking for work, but he might also be an outlaw with ideas about the bank and a posse on his backtrail.

As I passed the Silver Slipper, a big man with slicked-down hair and a small mustache suddenly appeared in the doorway. He wore a gray suit cut western style, a blue flowered vest adorned by a gold watch fob, and boots that probably cost more than I'd likely see in a year of riding herd.

A man whose face I couldn't make out moved in the darkness behind the big man, said something, and the expression on the big man's face went from idle curiosity to dark anger. He strode out onto the boardwalk and yelled at me. "Hey you, cowboy. I want to talk to you!"

The tone in his voice was that of a man used to giving orders and having them obeyed without question. Unless I was badly mistaken, I was about to meet Colby Ryan. Slipping the thong from my Colt, I turned Cap toward the boardwalk. I pulled up at the edge and hooked my leg over the saddlehorn.

"I'm Colby Ryan," he said. "I understand you killed one— I understand you killed a man outside of town this morning."

I smiled. "Way I look at it, he committed suicide."

"Huh? How do you figure that?"

"He drew on a loaded shotgun. If that isn't suicide, I don't know what is."

To my surprise, Ryan laughed. "You have a point, friend. I like a man who doesn't take chances. I'll give you a hundred a month and found. You start immediately."

"A hundred a month is fighting wages. You expecting a war?"

"What if I am? You don't look like a man who's afraid to fight."

"No, sir, but I'm real particular about which side I'm fighting for."

His face turned ugly. "What the hell does that mean?"

I shrugged. "I like to fight on the winning side, is all. I believe you're going to lose."

"*Lose!* Why, you ignorant cowboy, I've twenty top gun-hands working for me already. And all I'm up against is a handful of nesters. There's not a fighting man in the lot."

"Mister Ryan, you go in with that attitude and you'll likely be surprised real quick. Those men may be small ranchers—nesters, you call them—but I know at least one of them who was stepping on snakes before you started rattling."

For a moment his face went soft, everything except surprise gone. "I guess I was wrong about you," he said. "I figured you for a smart man."

"I never laid claim to being smart, but I know enough to ride clear of a skunk, and I think you're pure polecat. We've had our little talk, Mister Ryan, now I've some advice. Pull your horns in and be satisfied with what you already have.

"I don't know many people hereabouts, but the ones I do know, I count as friends. Leave them alone."

"And if I don't?"

"Then we'll have another little talk, only not so friendly. I won't come looking for your men, Ryan, I'll come to see you."

"Keep talking, cowboy. You may not be able to for long. I don't know where those nesters found you, but you better turn around and go back. Stay around Alamitos and one bright day somebody will jerk you from the saddle and pound some sense into your head."

"What's wrong with right now? I've heard you're a fighting man, Ryan. So far, all I've seen is a big mouth."

Ryan's face flushed and he took half a step toward me. Then he stopped short and looked quickly around. "No, not now. This isn't the time or the place. But keep your eyes open. One day you'll look around and I'll be there.

"You'd better give me your name, cowboy. You'll want it spelled right on your tombstone."

"Names don't mean much out here, Mister Ryan. We tend to judge a man by what he does rather than by who he is. But if you need a name, you can have one. My name is James Darnell.

"You go ahead and buy that tombstone, but don't go putting a name on quite yet. And be sure to pick one you like. Now, if you'll excuse me, the air is getting a little thick."

Touching the brim of my hat, I rode away, turning south on Station Street in order to get a look at the area south of the tracks. Glancing back toward the Silver Slipper as I turned the corner, I saw that Ryan was still standing on the boardwalk. His face had flickered at the mention of my name; it seemed certain he'd heard it before.

Well, that would cut no ice. I'd the reputation of being fast with a gun, and while that might make some men shy away, it would bring others on the run. But at least Ryan would know I wasn't bluffing and he might think hard before starting trouble.

Still, I wasn't taking him lightly in spite of my tough talk. Zeb Spencer was right when he called Ryan a fighting man. He was cold, smart, and dangerous. He might be wary enough to avoid an open war, but he could raise hob in other ways and it might not be easy to read him into the trouble. With rustling being a common problem, and with Alamitos full of men who would kill for a dime, Ryan might not have to make a move. He could sit back and let others do his dirty work, putting in a quiet hand behind the scenes to help things along.

Any way you looked at it, things were going to get real exciting before winter set in.

Within a few blocks the buildings on Station Street changed: wood and brick gave way to weathered adobe houses and shacks pieced together from discarded boards tacked together in an effort to keep out the rain and sun.

This went on for several blocks, then as I crossed the tracks near the cattle yard, prosperity of a different sort reappeared.

It was still a month shy of the time when most cattle drives would reach Alamitos, but already the cattle pens held more than two thousand steer, and dozens of railroad cars were being moved into position for loading them. I checked the brands on the cattle out of long habit and found that more than half were *Circle R*.

I'd have bet my summer wages that the *Circle R* was registered to one Colby Ryan.

I rode on, feeling out the town. The buildings again went from adobe to wood, though only a few were painted. Several saloons were already operating in spite of the early hour, and a brothel was having trouble keeping the flies out because of the steady stream of cowboys going in and out the door.

An old man with a big belly and tobacco-stained whiskers sat rocking in front of a barbershop. I pulled up in front of him, removed my hat, and wiped my brow with the sleeve of my shirt before speaking. "Nice day," I said.

He spat a stream of tobacco juice and knocked a fly sprawling. "It is and it ain't," he said. "If you've the price of a beer, it is. If you're sitting in a rocker wearin' the hide off your bottom wishing you had the price, it ain't."

I laughed and pulled a silver dollar from my pocket. "How would you like to earn this?"

He was a thirsty man and came half out of his chair. "Son, if you're funnin' me I'll whip you, old and wore-out as I am."

"I believe you would, but I'm not funning you. Just answer a couple of questions and she's yours."

"Fire away. If I don't know the answers I'll make 'em up as I go along."

"Fair enough. First question. Say a stranger wanted to find a saloon that served good food—the kind you can eat without worrying too much about it biting back—where would you go?"

"That's easy. If you want cheap, you go to the Cattleman. If you're looking to spend money, you go to the Silver Slipper. If you want plain good, why you go to Harry's Place or over to Rosie's, whichever happens to be closer.

"Harry's Place is two blocks down—that big sign stickin' out there."

"One more question. Suppose you didn't want to run into any of Colby Ryan's men while you were eating?"

He spat again. "Now that's curious. A stranger with a tied-down Colt wants to avoid anyone who works for Ryan. Generally they flock to him like wolves to a carcass. But to answer your question, he'd go to Harry's Place.

"Harry Morgan is a man with the bark on. He's been up the crick and over the ridge and none the worse for wear. He may have roped a horse or two that didn't belong to him, and some say he's mighty handy with any kind of weapon, but he's also a man who believes in skinnin' his own skunks, and he figures Ryan hires it done.

"There's no love lost between Morgan and Ryan, is what I'm trying to say. You want a quiet meal where you won't be bothered by Ryan or his men, you go to Harry's Place. Now, I've talked up a first-rate thirst. How 'bout that dollar?"

"You earned it." I flipped the dollar to him and he caught it on the rise. While I rode off toward Harry's Place, that old timer made a beeline for the Cattleman. He'd be wanting as many beers as possible for that dollar.

After tying Cap to the hitchpost in front of Harry's Place, I stepped through the swinging doors, pausing inside long enough to allow my eyes to adjust to the dim lighting. Truth is, there wasn't all that much to see.

Three men with bored looks on their faces played low-stake poker at a table near the window, and a half-drunk cowboy banged away at an old piano obviously in need of tuning. A bar stretched thirty feet across the far wall, and behind the bar a tall man with red hair and a neatly trimmed mustache wiped glasses with a rag.

It was cool inside, and in spite of the sawdust on the floor, the saloon was neater and cleaner than I'd expected. I walked to the bar and hooked a heel on the rail that ran along the bottom. The bartender looked me in the eye, glanced at my Colt, then at my right hand. He was a knowing man.

"Howdy, friend," he said. "What'll you have?"

"Beer," I said, "and anything you have to eat. If nothing's ready, just trot a steer out here and I'll swallow it whole . . . horns, hooves, and all."

He chuckled. "I've been hungry a time or two myself. We've beef, beans, and tortillas. Might even rustle up a couple of eggs, if the cook hasn't eaten them."

He drew me a beer, then walked through a doorway and gave my order to someone in the kitchen. I sipped the beer and was surprised to find it was cold . . . cold enough to freeze the fuzz off a peach. The bartender smiled. "Gets them every time," he said. "I got me an icehouse out back and she holds ice year-round. The Silver Slipper has the only other one. Good for business and doesn't cost much once you get it going."

I took a long pull of the beer and it went down smooth, clearing the trail dust from my throat and cooling me all the way to my heels. "You've a steady customer in me."

He drew me a second beer just as an old man with a gray, handlebar mustache and a three-day growth of beard came from the kitchen. The old man had three large plates on a tray, one piled high with beef and beans, a second holding a stack of tortillas, and the last filled to overflowing with half a dozen eggs smothered in chili. He set the plates on a table near where I stood and went back to the kitchen.

"That'll be one dollar for the food and two bits for the beer," the bartender said, "and cheap at twice the price."

I paid him before he could change his mind, sat down at

the table, and dug into the mounds of food. It was spicy, seasoned Mex style, and as hot as the beer was cold.

Eating such food is an art. First you shovel in a mouthful of beef and beans, loaded with hot peppers, and you chew until your teeth begin to melt. Next you swallow, quick, and chase it with beer and tortillas. The idea is to get the beer and tortillas to your stomach before the beef and beans burn a hole down to the soles of your feet.

I learned to like Mexican food while prospecting down Sonora way, and fifteen minutes after the old man set it on the table I was using the last tortilla to wipe the last plate clean. I leaned back, took a long drink of beer, lit a cigar, and belched. Maybe Alamitos wouldn't be so bad after all.

The bartender came around the bar carrying two glasses of beer. He gestured to the empty chair across the table from me. I shrugged and he sat down, sliding one of the glasses to me.

"This one's on the house," he said. "Name's Harry Morgan. You weren't lying when you said you were hungry."

"Just came up from Texas," I said. "I rode some lonesome country and never was much hand at cooking for myself."

I gave my name, and his eyebrows went up half a notch. "I've heard of you. They say you're the fastest man with a gun since Wild Bill. They also say you could carve a dozen notches on your gun if you wanted to."

"Stories get bigger with the telling," I said. "Fact is, I've killed six men, and only two of them when I had to be fast. It isn't a thing I'm proud of and I never went looking for a reputation. I do seem to have a knack for being in the wrong place at the right time."

He nodded slowly, his eyes on the past. "I know how it is. I've been lucky myself, but I grew up with a fellow who earned a rep as a fast gun. He really wasn't much good, but he killed a two-by-twice would-be badman in self-defense.

"The man he killed wasn't much good either, but after he was dead folks started talking like he was West Hardin or Jim

Courtright. It wasn't long before a real gunfighter came along with the idea of proving he was faster than my friend. And, of course, he was.

"I helped dig the grave, and I did my best to comfort his wife and children. Yes, sir, a rep's a bad thing to have unless you can back it up."

"It happens," I said. "About the only good that can be said of a rep is that once folks *know* you really are fast, they tend to leave you alone."

"Maybe, but you reach that point and it's wise to sit with your back to the wall. Look, you can figure this is none of my business, but I sat down here for a reason. I've a thing or two I'd like to know, and you can answer or not as you see fit.

"Thing is, you've got a reputation, and Colby Ryan is hiring every fast gun that rides in. You don't strike me as the kind who would work for Ryan, not if you knew anything about him, but if you do work for him, well, I don't want you back in here after today."

"That's hard talk," I said. "If I was working for Ryan, I might take offense and push you into a fight."

"You might, but it wouldn't be much of a fight."

He motioned toward the kitchen with a jerk of his head. I glanced that way and saw the old man who'd brought out my food. He was standing in the doorway and he held a Sharps .50-caliber buffalo rifle that could blow a hole in a man big enough for a drunken horse to stagger through. Morgan looked the other way and my eyes went with his. The cowboy who had been banging drunkenly away at the piano now looked cold sober . . . and he held a double-barreled shotgun.

I had to smile. "I like a careful man," I said, "but it isn't necessary. After today Colby Ryan is more likely to take a shot at me than to try to hire me again."

I told Morgan about the incident with Dancer and the run-in later with Colby Ryan. Taking a chance, I also told him why I was in Alamitos. It was risky being so free with information, but I wanted people to know right off where I stood, and I already knew that if Morgan wasn't on the right side, at least he wasn't on the wrong one.

"I know Zeb and Mary Kay," he said. "John Lysander, too. Zeb and John are both good men, but a little long in the tooth to be fighting the kind of trouble brewing around here.

"Dancer, huh? I never thought him to be any great shakes where smarts was concerned, but I didn't think he was stupid enough to draw on a shotgun. Well, he won't be missed.

"Funny you mentioning John. He usually stops in here every Friday night, regular as clockwork. I kept looking for him last night, but he never did turn up. First time in months he's missed a Friday-night poker game."

"Could be lots of reasons for that," I said. "You know how it is on a working ranch. Probably nothing to worry about."

"I know. I doubt John has more than two or three full-time hands right now, and I reckon that might make it hard to get away. Still, John is getting along in years, and between Ryan wanting his land, rustlers after his cattle, and plain damn bad luck . . . well, I'm worried is all."

I ran fingers through hair stiff with dust. "You may be right. I was going to find a bath and spend the night in a real bed before riding out to see John, but now you have me worried.

"The bath I got to have, but maybe I can find that bed out at John's. I should be able to get there by suppertime. I'm a man who likes his food."

"I noticed that," Morgan said. He drained the last of his beer. "You're taking a big job on your shoulders in helping John. Ryan is bad enough all by himself, but he isn't the only problem.

"Ryan is likely behind some of the rustling, and probably a few of the killings, but there's plenty of independents around, too. Anytime you have high cattle prices, easy trails to Mexico, and almost nothing in the way of law, you're going to have rustlers."

I slid my empty glass across the table. "John Lysander helped me once, and he never cared a damn what it might cost him. If there's anything I can do to square the account, then I mean to do it."

I stood up and put my hat on. Morgan described a route to Lysander's that was a little different from the one Zeb had given me. It was some longer, but would steer me well clear of Ryan's property and give me a better view of my backtrail in the process.

The first thing I did after leaving Morgan was find myself a bathhouse. Once there I eased into a tub of scalding water and just soaked for twenty minutes. It took another twenty to get the dirt and trail grime out of my hair, and ten more for a good, close shave.

After an hour I was as clean as I was likely to get. Putting on a clean shirt and fresh jeans that I had tucked in my bedroll, I gave that tub one last look. The water was clean when I got in, but after an hour of soaking it looked as if it could grow a pretty decent corn crop.

I left the bathhouse feeling like a new man. After lighting a cigar, I straddled Cap and rode south out of town, skirting close to the Malpais Lava Beds. In all my travels I'd seen nothing like those lava beds. They rolled across the country like a twisting snake, black, ugly and dangerous. The surface of the lava was sandpaper-rough and jagged edges were everywhere.

I'd heard talk that the lava beds concealed large tracts of grassland and that some of those areas were accessible if a man could find the trails and wasn't afraid to take a chance. It was a thing to keep in mind.

At last I found the trail that Morgan had told me about, and followed it south east. It had originally been a deer trail, widened over the years by cattle. It ran across the lower end of Cabolette Mesa and was supposed to take me directly to John's ranch house.

It did. Two hours after turning onto the trail I came to a

steep, shale-covered slope and saw a rambling ranch house in the clearing below. It was three hundred feet lower and two hundred yards distant from where I sat my horse, but I could see everything clearly.

One of the first things I saw was the body of a man sprawled facedown in the dirt not ten feet from the front porch.

CHAPTER 3

ALMOST without thinking, I turned Cap back the way we came and hunted cover. Tying Cap in a safe place, I slipped my rifle from the scabbard and dug out a spyglass given to me by my pa way back when. Pa took it off a Confederate officer who had no further need of seeing anything.

Taking the spyglass, I eased back to the edge of the slope on my belly, stopping as soon as I could see the ranch house. Training the glass first on the body, I breathed easier when I realized it wasn't John Lysander. The man was a stranger, but his hat had fallen off, revealing a mop of long, black hair. John's hair was cropped short and was snow white.

Four buildings—barn, stable, storage shed, and the main house—formed a half circle in the clearing, and I slowly examined each. They had obviously been built with an eye toward defense, and a man with a rifle in any one of the buildings could cover the other three.

That would be John's doing. He was a friendly man, but about as trusting as a turkey the day before Thanksgiving.

No light was visible in any of the buildings, and even the house seemed lifeless. The smallest trace of smoke came from the chimney of the house, but it was obviously from a dying fire. That worried me more than anything else.

A man pinned down in a house by a sniper would be a fool to risk a light, but he would still want a fire in the stove for cooking and warmth. Either the house was empty, or whoever was in there was in no shape to keep a fire going.

All right, if there was a sniper, and if he was still around, where would he be? The ridge where I lay was part of a series of foothills running the length of Cabolette Mesa. The foothills came up from the south, passed two hundred yards west of the ranch house, curled to the east, and came within a hundred yards of the nearest building before running off to the north again.

The curling hills would protect the house from a lot of wind and snow in hard weather, but they also offered a good bit of cover for a man who wanted to set an ambush.

I turned the spyglass back to the body and studied the ground around it. Two sets of faint tracks still showed in the soft earth, and they told a story. Two men had walked side by side from the house; only one had made it back.

Three feet from the body a splotch of blood stained the dirt, and more blood was visible on the porch itself. Near the bloody dirt was a skid mark where the second set of tracks doubled back to the house.

If I was reading the sign correctly, two men had walked from the house, and by the casual measure of the tracks, they were expecting no trouble. Someone had opened up with a rifle and one man, the one still in the ranch yard, was killed. The second man was wounded, but managed to reach the house before going down.

So one man, likely John, was in the house, possibly dead, but maybe wounded and needing help.

That would have to wait. Getting myself killed would help nobody. Before going down to the house I wanted to know where the shots had been fired from, and whether the man who fired them was still around.

I studied the ridge north of the house, not looking for a man so much as for any flicker of movement or anything out of place. Long minutes passed and I saw nothing. And then I got some help from an unexpected source.

The barn was visible at the edge of the spyglass's field, and though my attention was on the ridge, I saw a man suddenly appear in the wide doors of the barn. He wouldn't be visible from the ridge, but for all I knew he might be the killer trying to work closer to the house.

I trained the glass on him and watched. He was young and wore clothing typical of a working cowhand. He held a pistol, but I saw no rifle anywhere.

He took a couple of steps from the barn, then bolted and ran a zigzag course toward the house. A rifle opened up from the north ridge and a bullet kicked dirt between the running man's feet. He fell, then jumped back to his feet as a second bullet tore the hat from his head. He ran back to the barn, reaching it in a hail of bullets that miraculously left him untouched.

He hadn't reached the house, but he had uncovered the location of the killer. The rifle flashes came from the edge of a small clearing near the top of the north ridge. Studying the spot through the glass, I made out a hat first, then the vague shape of a man partially visible through the brush and trees.

I considered trying a shot from where I was, but quickly dismissed the idea. It was a long, difficult shot under the best of circumstances, and with the thick brush around the man the odds of the bullet being deflected were too great.

It was getting dark and whatever I was to do would have to be done soon. To complicate things, the sky had clouded over and a light rain was beginning to fall. Even as the first drops hit my back and sent shivers down my spine, the man on the ridge removed his hat and slipped an oilskin slicker over his head.

Well, at least he would stay warm and dry.

Easing back to my horse, I dug into the saddlebags again, replacing the spyglass and removing a pair of calf-high moccasins. Kicking off my boots, I pulled the moccasins on and wiggled my toes until they fit right.

What I had to do must be done quietly or not at all, and those moccasins would come in mighty handy before this night was over.

What bothered me most was the length of time that had passed since the man sprawled in front of the porch was killed. From what Morgan told me, it was probable the ambush had occurred yesterday evening as John was preparing to ride into Alamitos for his weekly poker game at Harry's Place.

It seemed unlikely that one man could have staked out the ranch for twenty-four hours. I'd seen no other sign of life except the young man who was being shot at and the man doing the shooting, but I was willing to bet that at least one other backshooter was up there, maybe at a camp on the far side of the ridge.

The more I thought about it, the more sense it made. While one man watched the house for a chance at finishing the wounded man, the second could be sleeping. In this way a round-the-clock watch was possible.

At any rate, that was how I intended to play it.

It was coming on to full dark when I began a slow, slow stalk around the back side of the ridge. It was raining harder and a cold wind was moving in with the rain, whipping the trees and brush into a frenzy. I had no slicker, but my shirt was made of buckskin and repelled much of the rain.

In many ways the storm was a blessing, even if a wet and uncomfortable one. Any noise I made would be covered by the fury of the storm, and that might give me an edge.

I walked slowly, letting my feet feel the way through the growing darkness. An hour after beginning the stalk I saw what I was looking for—the flicker of a campfire casting eerie shadows on the trees. I slowed even more, but continued forward until I was within fifty feet of the fire, pausing at that point to ponder things.

A lone man sat under a lean-to directly across the fire from me. He was drinking a cup of coffee and looking into the flames, apparently lost in thought. You'd think a man in his line of work would know better.

It's a damn-fool thing staring into a fire like that. When you look away from the fire and into the darkness you're night-blind for a minute or two, and that can spell the difference between living and dying.

I eased forward again, my moccasins making no sound on the wet ground. I was well within the firelight and no more than fifteen feet from the man when he looked up and saw me. His eyes snapped wide open and for a moment he froze, then dropped the coffee and went for his gun.

That moment of hesitation was all I needed. I crossed the space betweeen us in three long strides and swung my rifle from the hip. He was trying to stand up as he drew, and just as he reached his feet the metal butt plate on my rifle took him over the left ear. I felt bone crunch at the impact.

He went down in a heap, blood gushing from the side of his head. He opened his mouth, tried to speak, then his eyes glazed over and he died. I hadn't intended to kill him, but on the other hand, I didn't much give a damn, either. He'd picked up cards in a hard game and tried to raise when he should have folded.

A beat-up coffeepot sat on the fire, sizzling in protest each time a raindrop made it through the thick foliage above. Retrieving the cup dropped by the dead man, I swirled coffee in it as a rinse, then poured three-quarters of a cup and drank it quickly. It was scalding hot, pitch black, and strong enough to melt the horns of the devil himself. Just right.

Moving off into the shadows as I drank the coffee, I gave hard thought to waiting there for the second man to return. It likely would have been the smartest thing to do, but I just didn't have it in me.

It wasn't that he didn't have it coming, or that I was above turning the tables on him. Truth was, a man who would kill another from ambush was a man I wanted to meet as soon as possible . . . preferably over the sights of a rifle. What stopped me was impatience.

A few quick swallows of coffee had chased the chill from my bones, so I dropped the empty cup, checked the action of my rifle, and stepped off into the night. Somewhere out there was a man who had shot, maybe killed, John Lysander. Somewhere out there was a man who would either kill me or be killed himself. I wanted to see if he was up to shooting at a man who could shoot back.

CHAPTER 4

THE wind had blown a bucket of rain under the brim of my hat and down the back of my neck, and I was soaked from the waist down. I was tired, hungry, and getting mad. Moving faster, going up the back side of the ridge, I came down on the small clearing where I'd seen the dry-gulcher.

Pausing where the trees and brush abruptly thinned, I breathed easier and searched the darkness with eyes and ears. Long minutes passed with no sight or sound. Taking another step, a quick, careless one, my foot came down on a stick. It snapped, sounding unbelievably loud in the stillness.

Instantly a rifle roared and orange flame shattered the night from only yards away. Something tugged hard at the brim of my hat and I fired back, aiming at the flash, then firing left and right in case he moved. Without waiting to see if I'd scored, I dropped to the ground and rolled, coming up hard against the trunk of a huge pine.

A low moan floated through the air, but I wasn't about to move. If the man was hit, then waiting was in my favor. If he was pretending to be wounded all I'd have to do was move, come out from behind the tree, and he'd have the shot he wanted. I stayed where I was and waited. Ten minutes or more went by without another sound.

Staying behind the pine, I came to one knee for comfort and freedom of movement. Lightning cut across the night sky, momentarily turning night to day. We saw each other at the same time and fired as one. What happened to his bullet, I don't know, but in the split-second of light I saw his face erupt in a geyser of blood as the heavy bullet from my Winchester hit him in the bridge of his nose.

Blackness closed in again, followed by the thud of a body falling to the wet earth. I worked the lever, jacking another round into the chamber, and moved cautiously toward the fallen man. He was only a dark, irregular shape on the forest floor, and I held my rifle ready for a second shot while checking for a pulse.

There was no need for another shot. I struck a match and shielded it from the rain with a cupped hand. My bullet had badly distorted his face and taken off the back of his head, but I was certain I'd seen the man somewhere before.

That surprised me, but maybe it shouldn't have. I'd looked at a lot of wanted posters in my time, and a man who made his living shooting people from ambush likely had his face on a few.

Neither man proved to have a wallet or any identification on him, which didn't really surprise me. They were pros, but I checked their saddlebags anyway. The first held only the odds and ends such as piggin' strings, shaving kit, jerky, and ammunition that any man riding the range might carry. The other saddlebags held much the same, plus a fancy outfit for reloading rifle cartridges. There was nothing to give an identity to either man. That said a lot in itself.

Going back to my horse, I started down to the ranch. If John was wounded he'd need help and every minute counted.

I was in a hurry, but I hadn't lost all my senses, at least not yet. Stopping twenty-five yards short of the house, I called out, not wanting to be mistaken for one of the killers. There was no answer. Cutting the distance in half, I tried again. Still no answer.

I tied Cap to the porch railing, and took a minute to check the man sprawled in the dirt. He was dead. I stepped up to the cabin door, opened it slowly, and called into the darkness. There was no sound from within. Abandoning caution, I moved into the house and fumbled around in the dark and banged my shin twice before getting smart and striking a match.

Touching the match to a lamp, I adjusted the wick until the flame was right and looked around the room. Almost the first thing I saw was John Lysander. He was lying facedown on the floor next to an open window, blood pooling beneath his body.

He still clutched a rifle and a dozen or more empty cartridge casings strewn about the floor gave evidence that he'd somehow managed to put up a good fight before losing consciousness.

A whisper of sound came from behind me and a bit to my right. I stiffened and turned toward the sound, making no sudden movements of any kind. Just inside the door stood a man. He was wet, ragged, and dirty, but his eyes were the coldest gray I'd ever seen, and those eyes were looking at me over the barrel of a cocked Colt .45.

I eased my hands away from my side. "I'm a friend," I said.

His trigger finger whitened as he took up the slack. "You'd better be able to prove that," he said. "John Lysander was my boss, but he was also my friend and I'd like nothing better than to kill the bastard who killed him. You've just ten seconds to prove you ain't the man!"

"My name is James Darnell," I said. "I've a letter from John asking me to come and lend a hand."

His eyes flickered. "John mentioned your name. Take the letter out and lay it on the table, then back away."

I did as he said. He was just picking up the letter when John moaned softly and moved his hand. I darted across the room toward him. That fellow with the gun brought it up like he meant to use it. "John's alive," I said, "and I mean to help him. Either shoot or put that thing away and give me a hand."

He hesitated only long enough to read the envelope. He shoved his Colt back in the holster and we both ran to John.

I rolled John over on his back and opened his bloody shirt. There were two wounds, one low down on his right side and the other high in the chest. The one in his side had gone through and didn't look serious, though he'd lost more blood than he could afford.

It was the wound in his chest that scared me. The hole in his side I could handle, but the one in his chest was going to need a doctor. Soon.

"We've got to get him to a doctor," I said. "Go out and hitch up a wagon while I try to bandage these holes."

"All right, but are you sure he can stand a trip all the way to Alamitos? That's a long, rough ride in a wagon."

"To tell you the truth," I said, "I doubt it. But what else can we do? He needs help in the worst way."

"It's just an idea," he said, "but a man named Zeb Spencer has a ranch a ways from here. I've seen Zeb handle some pretty serious gunshot wounds, and it's only half the distance of Alamitos.

"Suppose I take John there while you go for the doctor. Seems to me we can get a doctor to Zeb's a lot quicker than we can get John to a doctor."

It made sense. "I know Zeb. Met him just today. You get the wagon ready and we'll do just that."

He started for the door. "Just a second," I said. "Seems I ought to know your name."

"It's Nolan Blocke," he said. Then he was out the door.

I hunted around until I found a clean cotton shirt and quickly cut it into strips. I would have liked to clean the bullet wounds with hot water, but there simply wasn't time. All I could do was wrap them tightly with the strips of cloth and hope the pressure would stop the flow of blood.

By the time I'd done all that was possible for John, Nolan had a wagon ready to go. He'd thought to put a layer of hay down to ease the ride, and we added to it by tossing a couple of quilts over that. We carried John out as gently as possible, placed him on the quilts, and covered him with a blanket.

I motioned to the dead man. "Who was he?"

"His name was Larry Stewart," Nolan said. "He just signed on with John a few weeks back. He was a good man."

Nolan climbed into the wagon seat and took the reins while I straddled Cap. When we were ready he pointed. "The quickest route to Alamitos is straight that way," he said. "It'll take you right across Colby Ryan's property, though, and he mightn't like it."

"To hell with Ryan," I said. "Just give me a path."

He nodded. "All right. If you push hard you should reach the railroad right-of-way in not much over an hour. There's a good road that will take you straight into Alamitos.

"I don't know how much trouble you'll have rounding up Doc Priter this time of night, but if you ain't back to Zeb's in four hours I'll come looking. Doc Priter may know the way to Zeb's, but it's awful easy to get turned around in this country after dark."

"I've ridden night trails a time or two," I said. "You just get John to Zeb's."

"One thing," he said. "I heard shots up on the ridge just as it was getting dark. None of the bullets seemed to come this way, so I figure you might have had something to do with it?"

"I'll tell you all about it later," I said. "Now you'd better get going. If you've a slicker you'd best keep it handy. It looks like more rain and that could kill John."

Nolan reached under the wagon seat and took out a oilskin tarp. "I'll keep him dry."

"Good. Let's move."

Nolan snapped the reins and clicked loudly. The horses lurched ahead and the wagon began to roll.

I touched Cap with my spurs and started off myself. It was rough, dangerous country and the best Cap could do at first was a trot. I pushed him as hard as I dared and we made decent time.

After a half hour or so I saw a flicker off to my right,

somewhat less than a mile away. The flicker became two tiny squares of light and I was pretty sure I was seeing the windows of a ranch house. If my bearings were right, that would be Colby Ryan's spread.

The urge was in me to ride over and tack his hide to the wall, but John came first. Ryan would have to wait, and as much as I hated to admit it, I had no proof he was behind John's being shot.

I pressed on and reached the road in just about the time Nolan had predicted. It was muddy and slick from all the rain, but there was far less danger of hitting a hole, so I pushed Cap harder. Then a streak of lightning ripped the sky apart and the rains came for real.

For fifteen minutes we kept going. Suddenly Cap's ears came up and he slowed to a walk. I'd trusted Cap's instincts before and he'd never let me down. Turning off the road, I cut Cap into a stand of trees and waited.

The *clop, clop, clop* of hooves smacking into the mud came to me before I saw anything. Then I saw two riders, nothing more than shadows in the darkness, coming down the road. They passed ten feet in front of us and one of them was cussing a blue streak. "Hell of a night to send a man out," he said. "I told the boss we wouldn't find him in Alamitos. If he'd done the job, he'd have come to get the rest of his money, wouldn't he?"

"I reckon," the other man said. "But he should've been back yesterday. Something's gone wrong and the boss ain't going to like it."

"What could've gone wrong? He had the perfect setup. Even I couldn't miss a shot like that, and he's supposed to be the best. And for the money he wanted, he'd better be."

"Maybe, but one thing I learned early on . . . there's always someone who's faster or better, and one day you're likely to meet him."

The riders faded into the darkness and their voices became inaudible. Waiting a couple of minutes to be safe, I urged Cap back onto the road. In twenty minutes we were in Alamitos and I was searching for a doctor.

A fellow about as drunk as anyone you ever saw gave me directions, but he was right. I went up the stairs to the doctor's office and pounded on his door. After a bit a light came on inside and the door opened.

Doctor Allen Priter was a tall man, middle-aged and thin as an old dollar, but I'll give him this: when I told him what was needed he didn't waste time asking questions. He grabbed his black bag, threw on a raincoat, and we headed for the stable at a good, fast trot.

He had a brand-new buggy and a fast-stepping sorrel to pull it. I tied Cap behind the buggy, climbed in beside the doctor, and we started for Zeb's ranch. It was still raining, but the buggy top offered a measure of protection. Doc Priter didn't seem to care one way or the other. He flicked the sorrel with his buggy whip, and she started off like it was race day and losing meant a trip to the glue factory.

We reached Zeb's ranch in less time than it had taken me to reach Alamitos, and once there the doctor got right to work. He went through the door, giving orders, and we all jumped to follow them.

Mary Kay already had water boiling, and Zeb was making bandages from a roll of cotton cloth. Doc Priter set me to rounding up nigh every lamp in the house and placing them near John. When everything was ready we all gathered round while the doctor examined John's wounds.

He bathed and cleaned both wounds and bandaged the one on John's side, then briefly probed at the hole in John's chest.

"It's bad," he said. "That bullet has to come out right now." He looked at Mary Kay. "Young lady, if you could lend a hand it would be a great help. The rest of you clear out."

John was pale, white as a ghost, and just looking at him scared me. "Is he going to make it?" I asked.

Doc Priter shrugged. "I don't know, and I won't know for

some time. We'll see. Now all of you clear out and let me get
to work."

John was in a back bedroom, so while Doc Priter and Mary
Kay went to work, the rest of us moved into the kitchen and
sat around the table. Me, I was about done in. I was wet to
the skin, cold to the bone, and I'd been running on have-to
most of the night.

Nolan looked to be in about the same shape, and I doubt
either of us could've jumped had we sat on a rattlesnake. Zeb
poured each of us a cup of coffee, and I don't think anything
ever felt better than the first gulp that I took. It was scalding
hot and I didn't care; its warmth spread slowly over me.

The kitchen was dimly lit and the cookstove was sending
out waves of heat. All three of us sat as still as dead men,
staring into our coffee and not saying a word, our minds
back in the bedroom with John. I nodded and must have
dozed, because when I opened my eyes Zeb was standing
over me with an armload of clothing.

"I ain't as big as either of you boys," he said, "but I reckon
these will fit well enough to sleep in."

"I might argue with you," Nolan said, "but I'm just too
dang tired."

We stripped from our wet clothing right there in the
kitchen and dug into the things Zeb gave us. A flannel shirt
and a pair of homespun pants proved a little tight, but no
worse than some clothing I'd owned over the years.

When we were dressed Zeb showed us a large room off the
kitchen. "Never hired enough help to need a bunkhouse,"
Zeb said, "so we always let the hands sleep here. You boys get
some rest and try not to worry about John. If there's any
change I'll wake you."

All I could do was nod. There were four cots in the room
and I took the second from the door. I would have taken the
closest, but Nolan beat me to it. Crawling under the covers
and dropping my head on the pillow, I yawned once. Then
I was asleep.

CHAPTER 5

WHEN I opened my eyes sunlight was streaming in the window and it must have been nigh seven in the morning. Sitting up groggily, I looked about the room and saw that Nolan was gone. Small wonder . . . I hadn't slept so late since I was old enough to walk.

Slipping into my boots and flipping my holster around my waist, I went into the kitchen. Zeb wasn't to be seen, but Mary Kay was busy at the stove and Nolan was sitting at the table. His hair was tousled and his eyes seemed a bit out of focus, so I reckon he hadn't been up long himself.

Mary Kay smiled and said good-morning when she saw me. She was bright-eyed and fresh, but I knew she must have had less sleep than any of us.

"Ought to be a law," I said.

Her brow wrinkled.

"I mean," I said, "that no one should be allowed to look so pretty after a night like you had."

She smiled. "You start talking like that," she said, "and I might start thinking you're courting me."

I felt the blood rush to my face. "Well, ma'am," I said, "I can think of worse fates."

"Oh, you can? That's very generous of you. Now hush and sit down. Breakfast is almost ready."

I hushed and sat down. "How's John?" I asked.

Mary Kay suddenly looked grim. "Gramps is sitting with him now. Doc Priter left only an hour or so ago. I don't know, but it doesn't look good."

"I talked to the doc for a minute before he left," Nolan said. "The way he put it, it's all up to John. He lost a god-

42

almighty lot of blood, but if he's tough enough, he just might make it."

"Then he'll make it," I said. "When it comes to being tough, John wears out his clothes from the inside."

Mary Kay started covering the table with platters of eggs, bacon, hot biscuits, and gravy. "Doc Priter got that bullet out slick as you please," she said. "I tried to help, but I don't ever want to go through that again."

"It took nerve to be there at all," Nolan said. "Nobody ever said I was anything but rawboned and rough, but I'll tell you, I'm glad it was you in there instead of me."

"Amen," I said.

Mary Kay set a pot of coffee on the table and we all dug in. I reckon Nolan and me did most of the damage, but Mary Kay managed to put away her share. Seemed like I'd just got started when I reached for another biscuit and came up empty. I was able to get the last piece of bacon, but nearly got Nolan's fork in my hand in the effort.

After pouring another cup of coffee, I went in to check on John. He was still unconscious, but seemed to be breathing easier and wasn't so pale.

"He tried to say something once or twice," Zeb said. "He has a long road ahead, but I think he just might make it."

"I hope so. If he doesn't, Ryan best hunt a hole."

"You got to have proof," Zeb said. "You go off half-cocked and you'll put yourself on the wrong side of the law. Colby Ryan is a snake, but he has connections."

I knew Zeb was right, but it rankled me. I never was much good at going through channels, and when a snake reared up and threatened to strike, it seemed a good idea to discourage it . . . and the best way to do that was a well-placed bullet.

Zeb and me talked for a minute about what had happened up on the north ridge and it gave me an idea. "I'm going to ride over and take those bodies into town," I said. "Maybe that'll stir things up a bit."

Zeb smiled. "If it don't, nothing will. But you go careful, and watch out for Burack. Ryan runs that man and you'll have to take those bodies to him."

I nodded and went out. Nolan was still in the kitchen, but Mary Kay was nowhere to be seen. I told Nolan what I intended to do and asked if he wanted to ride along.

"I'll go as far as the ranch," he said. "I want to bury Stewart proper, then I'd like to have a look around. I came up way short on the herd count, and I want to know why."

"How short?"

"Hard to tell before roundup, but John should have better than two thousand head of branded cattle. Unless I'm badly mistaken, I doubt there's more than a thousand left.

"Of course, that's wide-open country. There're draws and gulleys everywhere and no fences to be seen, so anything that's wandered onto Ryan's land is gone. Still, we were pretty regular in pushing the herd toward the southern half of the range. We did a count not more than two months ago and it came out pretty well. But all of a sudden I have to burn the brush and rake the ashes just to find a cow."

"You think it's rustlers?"

"More'n likely. But if it is, they had to leave sign and I mean to find it."

"Sounds good," I said, "but if you do find it, don't go following any trails alone. Hunt me up and we'll go read those thieves the law together."

"I'm no hero," he said. "I can't rightly remember ever being scared, but there was a time or two when my feet disagreed with my head on which way to go. You want to tag along and lend a hand, why, I'll be glad to wait just as long as it takes. Besides, the way rustlers work in these parts, there should be enough to go around."

We both changed into our own clothes, and I took the time to shave while Nolan saddled the horses. Cap was as tired as I was and Nolan's horse was over to John's, so he picked two of Zeb's best for us.

I finished shaving and dabbed a little whiskey on my face, wincing at the sting. Looking myself over in the mirror, I sadly shook my head. My hair was too long and I had a scar along the underside of my chin from an Apache bullet that near ruined more than my pride.

No doubt about it, I wasn't going to win any prizes for looks, but at least with the whiskers scraped off nobody would mistake me for a grizzly. I put on my hat and walked out into a bright, cool morning.

The rain had moved on, and the sky was bright blue and dotted with white, fluffy clouds. It looked like a fine morning all the way around . . . until I straddled that big gelding Nolan was kind enough to pick for me. Somebody forgot to tell that horse it wasn't a stallion anymore.

I've sat astride a bucking horse a time or two, but this one was serious. We went up and down and around that corral for a good five minutes before the horse decided I was in the saddle to stay. When it did stop, it was all at once. It walked me out of there polite as you please, snapping its head around once and giving me a look that seemed to say, "Okay, you can ride a little, but just you wait till next time."

Nolan was laughing so hard he liked to have fell off his own horse. Me, I just rode away and left him there. He caught up after a few minutes, but every time I glanced his way the corners of his mouth started having trouble, so I did my best just to ignore him.

We were a quarter mile from the ridge that overlooked John's ranch house when we both smelled smoke. I looked at Nolan and he looked back, then we stuck the spurs to our horses. Topping the ridge, we went down the other side on the fly, not caring what we ran into.

We were too late. The barn was nothing but a pile of smoldering ashes. The house had been set on fire, but the job was hastily done and only a couple of logs at one end were charred. "Too lazy to go in and do it right," I said. "Lucky for the rain or it might have been enough."

"They did the barn up proper," Nolan said. "Didn't even let the stock out first, and one of the horses in there was mine. I figure I owe somebody for this one."

We scouted around and studied the tracks. There had been at least four riders, maybe five, and while the tracks were mostly washed out by the rain, a few were distinct. We studied them carefully, looking for anything that might allow us to identify them later, such as the size of the horseshoe print or any unique scratches and nicks in the shoe.

It was such a sign we sought; we found it quickly. One of the horses, probably a mustang by the size, had a right front shoe that was thicker and heavier than the left. This was usually done to keep the horse from swinging that hoof too wide, giving it a smoother, steadier, and faster gait.

A second, much larger, horse had a big, star-shaped nick in one of its shoes. The two remaining prints were made by shoes too new to have much in the way of nicks or scratches, but we'd know those first two wherever and whenever we came across them.

Nolan had a hard look on his face. "If you want to go after them," he said, "just say the word."

I slowly shook my head. "No, the trail's too old and we have other things to take care of. Don't worry, we'll meet up with them sooner or later."

"You can count on that," Nolan said. "That horse of mine was ugly as sin and ornery as hell, but he carried me out of more trouble than I could ride into."

I knew how Nolan felt. Out in that country a man's horse was often worth his life. I could recall a half dozen times when one horse or another had saved my hide, and had Cap been in that barn I'd have gone hunting hair.

I removed my hat, wiped my brow, settled my hat back in place, and scanned the countryside. It was peaceful now, but with John out of the way, Ryan might be tempted to move in. "I know you work for John," I said, "but we need a man or two who can stay right here at the ranch full-time. I'd better hire a couple if I can find men we can trust."

Nolan took a long drink from his canteen. "That barn is proof we need somebody here," he said, "while I'm out and about. I can think of a couple of good ol' boys who might fill the bill. Brothers, Jeff and Joe Coger. They spend about half their time prospecting and the other half fighting. It isn't that they hunt trouble, but both of them are rough as a cob and they won't backwater for any man. I reckon they could use the money, and I know they'd like a chance to buck Colby Ryan."

"Sounds good. Where can I find them?"

"Now that might be a problem," he said. "Like I told you, they put in a lot of time prospecting, and they tend to work in the lonesomest country in the territory.

"They don't go in for savin' money, though, and when they get a little put back they drift into town and stay until it's gone. Just have to ask around."

"I expect it'll raise a ruckus when I haul those bodies in, but I'll take a stab at finding them if I have the time. What are you going to do?"

Nolan shrugged. "Sift the south range and look for some sign of cattle thieves. Most rustlers take fifteen, twenty head and push them out of the country before anyone's the wiser. But by my guess, we're missing at least three hundred maybe five hundred head. That many cattle will leave a trail somewhere."

"All right, but go careful. That's a lot of cattle to hide and it's certain they'll have it well guarded."

"I'll go easy. I almost hate to ride out, though—I'd sure like to see the look on Ryan's face when you ride in with those stiffs over the saddle."

The only thing left to do was bury Stewart. We wrapped his body in a blanket from the cabin and carried him to a pretty knoll not far away. After we buried him, I spoke a few words I rememberd from the Good Book. When it was over, I looked at Nolan. "Did he have any family?" I asked.

"None that he mentioned," Nolan said. "I don't even know where he drifted in from."

We walked back to the cabin, both of us silent. A lot of good men came to the same end as Larry Stewart, and each of us knew it could happen to us.

We saddled up and Nolan rode off, waving a hand as he did so. I'd told him to go careful, but the truth is I didn't worry much about Nolan Blocke. Anybody tangling with him was going to lose some hide.

Turning my horse to the north ridge I went up slow, finding both bodies where I left them. There was no sign that anyone had been nosing around in the time I'd been gone, but I went mighty easy just the same. Somebody had sent those two to kill John, and when they didn't come back, it would raise questions.

Only when I was absolutely certain that the area was free of unwanted intruders did I move to the bodies and set about making them ready for the trip back to town.

I threw both bodies over their horses, tied them down, then started off toward Alamitos. I took my Colt out and checked the action, then slid it in and out of the holster a few times to be certain it wouldn't snag. I had to be ready for anything because taking those bodies into Alamitos was likely to stir up a king-size hornet's nest.

Up till now, Ryan had things going pretty much his own way. Now he would know he was in a war, and he wasn't about to back down and be a good boy. Unless I missed my guess, those bodies would bring things into the open. This county was headed for a war and it would soon be choose your side and pick your target.

I'd been around range wars before, and there was nothing pretty about any of them. People were killed, the innocent as well as the guilty, and being right didn't mean much. Bullets don't come with names written on them, and I'd seen too many good men killed to believe in any special providence protecting me.

In a range war, the winner is the last man standing when the smoke clears. If you want to know who came in second, all you have to do is check the markers on boot hill.

That's what was coming and we weren't set up for it. Ryan had too many guns and would undoubtedly hire more. I wasn't sure how many guns would be on our side, but I did know we'd be outnumbered at least three or four to one, and probably more.

Yet in spite of the odds, there had to be something I could do. If a man looks sharp enough he can always see a way to even things out a bit, and that's what I had to find . . . a way to even the odds and put Ryan on the defensive.

CHAPTER 6

FOLKS must have seen us coming a ways off, because I'd barely reached the edge of town before a crowd started forming. People followed alongside me and the corpses, whispering among themselves; a few shouted questions.

Of course, those two coyotes tied over their saddles didn't say scat to anyone, and neither did I. I looked straight ahead and kept my mouth closed until I was in front of the marshal's office.

No one came out, so I caught the eye of a man in the crowd. "Any idea where the marshal is?" I asked.

A rough voice sounded off to my right and the crowd parted like a wave. "I reckon that'll be him coming now," the man said, then added a warning. "Watch yourself. He's in a foul mood."

I nodded and the man backed into the throng. Smart fellow, that one. As often as not it's the innocent bystander who gets hurt when there's trouble. It takes a wise man to back off and hunt cover before trouble starts.

Burack pushed through the crowd and stomped onto the boardwalk in front of me. "What's going on here?" he bellowed. He jabbed a finger at the bodies. "What's that?"

"I guess you might say it's the wages of sin," I said. "These boys transgressed against the straight and narrow and reaped what they tried to sow."

"Huh? What kind of fool talk is that?"

"You should spend more time in church," I said, "but I'll make it real simple for you. They shot John Lysander and another man, from ambush. I took exception."

"You killed both of them?"

50

"They wouldn't have it any other way. Both of them tried to shoot me."

Burack swore. "I guess you have witnesses to back your story?"

"All you want."

Burack looked around at the crowd. He seemed at a loss as to what he should do next. "I'll have to take your gun until we get to the bottom of this," he said at last.

"Like hell."

"What!"

"Like hell," I repeated. "I brought these men in of my own free will. I could just have easily left them in the woods to rot and no one the wiser."

Burack's face turned red. "I'm the marshal here, and if I want your gun, then by God I'll have it."

"In the first place, *Marshal*, this happened outside your jurisdiction. . . ."

Burack's eyes kept looking into the crowd off to my left. I looked that way and saw Colby Ryan. He was looking at Burack, and I saw him almost imperceptibly nod his head. Burack nodded back and slipped the thong from his Colt.

"I'm the marshal," Burack said again, "and if I want your gun I'll take it."

The horses carrying the dead men had walked up beside my own, and a thick, heavyset man was looking at the bodies. He grabbed the hair of the one I'd shot and raised the ruined face up to get a better look.

"You'd best look at your hole card, Marshal," he said. "I don't know the other gent, but this one is Vince Trible. That bullet didn't improve his looks none, but it's him."

A murmur went through the crowd, and small wonder. Vince Trible was a name known far and wide, discussed in saloons and around lonely campfires in the same breath with Jesse James or Cole Younger. He was a hired killer and said to be at the beck and call of anyone who could afford him. And he didn't come cheap.

That face had looked familiar, but I hadn't placed it. Now that I heard the name, however, I remembered seeing a wanted poster on him some years before.

Burack never flinched at the name, and I was pretty sure he'd known all along who was draped over the horse. "I don't care who it is," he said. He looked back at me and I knew he intended to push me into a fight.

Well, if he wanted it, he could have it. Killing a marshal, even a crooked one, could put me in a lake of hot water, but allowing myself to be locked up in a town controlled by Colby Ryan was as good as signing my own death warrant.

My pa always said it was better to be born lucky than smart, and at that moment I got lucky. Three men pushed through the crowd and stepped onto the boardwalk. "Maybe you don't care who the dead men are," one of them said, "but we do. Vince Trible was a murdering skunk and I'd say every honest man in the territory owes this man a debt of gratitude for killing him."

"That ain't the point," Burack sputtered. "I'm the marshal here and it's my job—"

"It's your job to take care of things in town," the newcomer broke in. "And as this gentleman so aptly pointed out, this did not take place in town."

He turned to me. He was tall, well set up, graying at the temples, but not over thirty-five or so. "My name is Aaron Van Dorn," he said. He nodded at the two men with him, one a short, powerfully built Mexican and the other an average looking, potbellied man of about sixty. "This is Brigo Juarez and Robert Schmidt. The three of us, along with Mayor Gribbins, comprise the town council of Alamitos. As I said, I believe we owe you a debt of gratitude, Mr . . ."

"Jim Darnell," I said.

"That name sounds familiar. You were a shotgun guard for Wells Fargo, weren't you?"

"Among other things."

"Uh-huh, I thought so. At any rate, I believe you have a sizable reward coming for bringing Trible in."

"I didn't shoot him for money," I said.

He glanced at Burack. "I know, but if you don't claim the money someone else might."

A movement caught the corner of my eye, and I turned in time to see Colby Ryan skulking quietly away. He didn't look any too happy. I'd been there long enough myself. "Thanks for your help, Mr. Van Dorn," I said. "If there's nothing else, I'll be moving along."

"There is a thing or two. First, about that reward?"

I didn't want the money, but he was right about Burack putting in a claim if I didn't. "Does John Lysander have an account at the bank?" I asked.

"I would imagine so," Van Dorn said. "Most all the ranchers do."

"When the money comes through, put it in his account. That's the least Trible, and whoever hired him, can do. And that reminds me, I've a few thousand dollars I took off Trible and his partner. What should I do with it?"

"As far as I'm concerned," Van Dorn said, "you may as well keep it. Money like that is tainted. Use it to do some good. As to the account, I'll see to it personally. Just one more thing. Will you still be in town this evening?"

"It's possible."

"I believe the three of us, along with the rest of the council and the mayor, would like to see you. The mayor's office?"

"All right."

"Say four or a bit after. Don't worry about these bodies. I think the marshal can find a place for them."

Burack scowled, but made no reply. Tipping my hat, I rode away. The crowd parted to let me through, and I urged Cap into a trot. The story of my bringing Vince Trible in belly-down on a horse would spread like wildfire and I wanted to hunt a hole for a few hours.

Harry's Place was about the only choice I could think of

and I went straight there. When I went in the swinging doors Harry raised a hand in greeting. He drew me a beer and shook his head when I started to pay him.

"Your money's no good today," he said. "It's the least I can do for the man who killed Vince Trible."

My mouth opened in surprise. "How'd you know about that?" I asked. "I rode straight here from Burack's office."

"You know how it is," Morgan said. "Nothing travels as fast as a good story. I reckon you're the most talked-about man in the country right now."

"I don't mind being talked about," I said, "but that kind of talk can get a man killed." But it didn't do much good to worry, however, and I'd plenty of more immediate concerns to keep me busy. The first order of business was to locate the Coger brothers. I asked Morgan about them and he smiled.

"Sure," he said. "I guess everybody in this part of New Mexico knows those boys.

"Good men, the both of them. Just a little rambunctious, is all. They'll fight anybody at any time for any reason, and if nobody else is about, they'll fight each other."

"Any idea where I can find them?"

He smiled. "Yeah, I can tell you where to find them. Right now they're cooling their heels in jail. They got to feeling their oats a few nights back and decided to pay a visit to the Silver Slipper. Whilst there they made the mistake of sitting in on one of Ryan's poker games.

"Jeff's the older by a year, but he ain't one tad cooler. He spotted some cardsharp dealing from the bottom of the deck and took exception to it. Now, either of those boys can handle a gun slick as goose grease, but they prefer their fists.

"That sharpie tried to draw a hideout gun when Jeff called him down, so Jeff just naturally laid a big five alongside that fellow's jaw. They went to swinging at anything that moved and started a free-for-all that must have been something to see.

"I wasn't there myself, but a fellow who was told me that

Jeff and Joe stretched out near a dozen men before Burack showed up and trotted them off at the end of a shotgun."

"Sounds like just the kind of men I had in mind. How long will they be in jail?"

"Near four months unless somebody pays their fines. Fact is, I planned on getting them out, but I wanted to let 'em sweat a week or so. I owe them a favor or two, but they've picked a fight in here more than once and I figured some time behind bars might make 'em think things over."

"It might at that, but I need them out now."

He reached for his wallet. "Like I said, I'd have bailed them out myself in a few days. I'd take it kindly if you'd let me pay their fines anyway."

I waved him off. "Thanks, but I have enough to cover it. Besides, I'll take it back out of their wages. That should teach them some kind of lesson."

"It might at that. I'll give you a hint about the Cogers, though. Like as not they'll talk tough when you first ask them about working for you. It'll be good-natured, but they'll want to size you up. Give back as good as you get and don't lose your temper. They're fighting men and they respect other fighting men. You're good with a gun, but they might want to know if you're willing to use your fists."

"I'll keep it in mind."

I hung around Harry's Place until after the noon meal, then spent a couple of hours wandering around the stock-yard and getting to know Alamitos a little better. At three I rode to the jail, thinking to bail the Cogers out and then go to the meeting with the town council.

I'd spent a good bit of the day thinking about that meeting. I worried at it like a dog worries at a bone, in fact, but I could think of no good reason why they should want to see me. At last I shrugged mentally and gave it up. They'd tell me what they wanted at four, and I could answer yes or no when I knew more about it.

Burack was in his office and he was in a foul mood. He was

just tipping a bottle of whiskey when I walked through the door. When he saw me he jerked in surprise, spilling whiskey on the front of his shirt and near dropping the bottle in the process. He jumped to his feet and wiped at his shirt with a dirty bandanna. "What the hell do you want?" he snarled.

"Understand you have a couple of men locked up," I said. "I'd like to talk to them."

"I've half a dozen locked up. Which two did you have in mind?"

"Jeff and Joe Coger."

"Huh, those troublemakers? What do you want with them?"

"Like I said, I want to talk to them, and if I like what they have to say I might want to pay their fines."

The marshal got ten percent of any fines, so that quieted Burack down some. "It's a waste of good money if you ask me," he said, "but it's your money."

He led me into the back of the jail and down a line of cells. The Cogers were in the last cell by themselves, and they were a sight. They looked like brothers, all right, and they looked like men who could fight. Both were over six feet, well muscled and blond.

Both of them also wore good-natured, go-to-hell expressions on their faces. One of them had a black eye and the other nursed a bruised and swollen cheek, but they were in pretty good shape, all things considered.

They were stretched out on their cots, and the one with the black eye swung to a sitting position as we stopped in front of the cell.

"What you got there, Marshal?" he said. "You all catch yourself a real badman this time?"

"I'd be nice to him," Burack said. "He tells me he might want to bail you out."

At this point both men came to their feet and approached the cell door. "What'd you want to do that for," the one with the lump on his cheek asked. "I don't know you from Adam."

"Which brother are you?" I asked.

"Jeff," he said. "This here is Joe."

"Well, I'll tell you, Jeff," I said. "I'm working for John Lysander and he's laid up. We need somebody to live at the ranch and keep an eye on things. I need a couple of gentle souls who won't go too hard on any night riders that happen by, and Nolan Blocke and Harry Morgan both claim you fill the bill.

"Morgan, he said there weren't two more peaceable fellows to be found. In fact, he said neither of you could whip his weight in schoolboys, but I told him that was all right."

I said all that with a straight face and the Coger boys were a sight. Their mouths dropped open, they looked at me, at each other, at the marshal, then back at me. They didn't know whether I was serious, or just plain soft in the head.

Joe's face turned beet red and he got mad. "Why you long-legged, mule-eared yahoo, let me out of this cell and we'll see who can fight!"

I smiled. "You? Why, I'd knock you so far you'd be an old man before you could ride back."

His mouth dropped open and he looked at his brother, then back at me. His brother chuckled. "Ain't often somebody gets the last word in with Joe," he said. "I reckon you got to be James Darnell . . . the fellow who brought in Vince Trible?"

"That's right."

"Well, boss, get us out of here. You hired yourself a couple of hands."

Burack didn't move. "I'd advise against it," he said to the brothers. "This jasper has come out lucky so far, but he's bucking a stacked deck and sooner or later he'll lose the pot. You boys go to working for him and you might wind up in more trouble than the pair of you can handle."

Jeff looked at his brother. "Joe, you scared?"

"Not so you'd notice."

Burack shrugged. "Your funeral. Just a friendly warning, is all. No skin off my nose either way."

Burack turned to me. "You got a hundred dollars?"

I near choked. "That's a little steep for fighting, isn't it?"

"You got to figure in the damages," Burack said, "and they're getting off easy. You want 'em, it'll cost you a hundred dollars."

I paid him, got a receipt, and took the Coger brothers outside. "You two ride out to the ranch and settle in," I said. "I've business in town yet, but I'll try to check in on you time to time."

"Just what is it you expect us to do out there?" Joe asked.

I explained all that had happened at the ranch. "You get any riders by night," I said, "you let them know the Lysander ranch is private property and ask them to leave."

"What if they refuse?" Jeff asked.

"Persuade them. And don't take chances. Give a warning if you can, but don't say it twice. If things get rough, shoot to kill."

They rode out and I didn't worry about them. Those boys had the bark on and didn't know the meaning of quit. Anybody who came around the ranch looking for trouble while the Cogers were there would get exactly what they deserved.

I took my hat off, ran fingers through my hair, and resettled the hat on my head. All that remained was to see the town council, and I wasn't looking forward to that. I didn't know what they wanted, but it was likely something that would cost me in one way or another.

Aaron Van Dorn was an impressive man, and likely a good one, but his main interest was in the welfare of Alamitos, and not in James Darnell's. Not that I held that against him, but it did mean I'd have to keep my eyes open and think twice about anything he said.

But guessing wasn't going to get me anywhere. The only way I'd know for certain what they wanted was to go and see.

CHAPTER 7

I FOUND the mayor's office and went through the door. A plump, attractive women of about forty greeted me. She asked my name, smiled brightly, and led me into the council chamber.

Five men were in the room: Van Dorn, Juarez, Schmidt, and two others I hadn't seen before. Van Dorn shook my hand.

"It was good of you to come, Mr. Darnell," he said. "You remember Brigo Juarez and Robert Schmidt?"

I shook hands with them and Van Dorn introduced the other two men. The first was sixty or so and just ten pounds shy of fat. He was seated at the head of a long conference table and rose with a grunt to shake my hand. "This is Mayor Gribbins," Van Dorn said. He then turned to the last man at the table. "And last but not least, this is Chester Watkins. Chet is president of the bank."

Watkins was a tiny man with a long nose and thin lips. He was dressed in a severe black suit and wore wire-rim glasses. He made no move to rise or shake my hand.

The door to the room opened behind me and I turned to see Doc Priter. He raised a hand in greeting. "Good," Van Dorn said, "I believe we're all present now. If everyone will take his seat we can get down to business."

I sat down at the end of the table opposite Mayor Gribbins. Doc Priter was to my right and Juarez to my left. Before we got started Doc Priter asked me about John. "He was still unconscious when I left this morning," I said, "but he seemed to be breathing easier and his color was better."

"That's a good sign," he said. "John lost a lot of blood and he was in shock, but every minute he hangs on increases his chances. I'll come out and check on him in the morning. By then his wounds will need to be cleaned and the bandages changed.

Van Dorn cleared his throat. "We may as well get to it," he said. "Since most of this was his idea, I'll gladly let Mayor Gribbins do the speaking."

The mayor leaned forward and began to speak with a voice that sounded like it was filtered through wet gravel. "Until now," he began, "this has only been a wish and a want. We could talk about it, but had no power to act. All this has changed."

"All what has changed?" Watkins asked. "I don't have the faintest idea what you're talking about."

"If you will give me a minute," Mayor Gribbins said, "I'll make it all perfectly clear.

"As you are all well aware, we have experienced a great deal of violence and theft in and about Alamitos the last couple of years, and it continues to increase at a frightening rate. Most of us believe Colby Ryan is behind some measure of the trouble, but he is far from the only concern.

"We have enough rustlers, thieves, murderers, card sharps, and prostitutes to corner the market, and all we have on the side of law and order is a town marshal who is either a lackey for Ryan or merely a man of such low character that he cannot or will not keep the peace. Either way, something must be done."

"If I understand you," Watkins said, "we are discussing the firing of Marshal Burack and the hiring of a new man. Isn't this a bit theatrical for so simple a task?"

"It might be if you were correct," Mayor Gribbins said. "We do intend to fire Marshal Burack, but the position of town marshal will no longer exist. The man we replace Burack with will be a *county* sheriff. He will be able to enforce the law throughout the county, and when actually in close pursuit, follow a trail out of the county."

Doc Priter whistled. "Can we do that? I thought the position of county sheriff was to be located in the county seat."

"That is correct," Van Dorn said. "And as of, let's see, roughly thirty-six hours ago, Alamitos is the county seat."

Doc Priter's mouth opened wide and Watkins nearly choked. "Why, that's great," Doc Priter said. "But how? Why?"

"It wasn't really that difficult," Mayor Gribbins said. "It was inevitable that as this area grew, a county seat would have to come into being. The question was always which town would be it. Since Alamitos has grown at such a rapid rate over the last five years, well, we were the logical choice.

"I will admit, however, that one of the things we had to promise was to get the violence under control. A lot depends on this."

"Quite a lot," Van Dorn said. "You see, county seats may be changed by a vote of all residents of said county. Within four years a county-wide vote will be taken, and should Alamitos still be considered a wild and woolly boomtown the vote will quite likely go against us."

Me, I'd been listening to it all and a terrible suspicion was growing in my gut. I'd heard plenty, in short, and figured it was time to do some speaking. "What does all of this have to do with me?" I asked. "I know very little about county seats or politics. I'm not even a resident here."

"Not yet," Mayor Gribbins said, "but you have been a Wells Fargo guard and a deputy sheriff. You have the reputation of being fast with a gun, but also of always using your gun on the side of law and order.

"What we want from you, Mr. Darnell, is your expertise and your character. We want you to accept the position of county sheriff."

I took a deep breath and let it out slow. "I'll be absolutely honest with you," I said, "and I doubt you'll like it. Yes, I have worn a badge, but there was very little about it that I liked.

"To begin with, a badge makes too good a target. Even in a two-bit town where the worst thing that happens is some drunk shooting up the town, even there you're a target. In a town like Alamitos you might as well paint a big sign on your chest that says "Shoot me.""

"But the thing is this, I came here to help John Lysander out of a tight spot. That's my priority. Being sheriff might interfere with that."

Mayor Gribbins rubbed a beefy hand over his eyes. "Look," he said, "I can understand your feelings, but this is a good town and it needs help. I think you happen to be the best man for the job, and I also think you know it.

"As for being a target, aren't you one anyway? Colby Ryan is only going to let you meddle for so long before he decides it would be in his best interests to have you killed. Also, if you want to help John Lysander, what better way than to do it through the office of sheriff?"

"There is another point to consider," Doc Priter put in. "I've been around a bit in my time, and this situation isn't completely new to me. From my experience I can tell you this, sooner or later the law will come to Alamitos, if not by what we do here today, then by outside forces such as a United States marshal.

"When that happens things will be frozen in place. What I mean is this, if Colby Ryan has the upper hand and is viewed as a respectable rancher, then the law will come in on his side, no matter what people think of him privately. Anyone going against Ryan, particularly an outsider, might suddenly be considered an outlaw. That is something to consider, Mr. Darnell. If you aren't wearing a badge, the day may come when you are pursued by one."

Doc Priter had touched one of my worries. I'd been around more than a bit myself, and I knew it was exactly as he said. If too much rustling and murder occurred within this area, sooner or later the governor would be forced to

act. He would send in the U.S. marshals or the army, and
they would clean it up.

But they would be coming in cold, unaware of the whole
picture. They would see Colby Ryan as the largest, most
prosperous rancher in the county, and they would see me as
an outside gun hired to fight him. That would be an easy
way for me to end up on the wrong side of the law. It had
happened before and could happen again.

"I'll tell you what," I said. "I'd like to mull things over
before deciding anything, so if it's all right, I won't say yes or
no just now. Give me a few days to think it over and I'll give
you an answer."

Chet Watkins's face was pinched into a disapproving mask
. . . he looked like a weasel with constipation. "I believe this
whole thing is ill-conceived," he said. "It is good news that
Alamitos is now the official county seat. It should bring some
profitable business and investment money our way, but I
don't think we should stir things up by having Mr. Darnell,
or anyone else, run all over the county with a badge on his
chest. That is the very last thing we need."

"To the contrary," Juarez said, "it is exactly what we need.
I may not know as much of the law as some of you, but I do
know about rattlesnakes, and that's what we are dealing with
here . . . a den of rattlesnakes in our very midst.

"To get rid of a den of rattlesnakes you stir them up with
dynamite, then step on their heads when they come into the
light."

No one said much after that, though I did ask again for a
few days to decide on the job of county sheriff.

"We've waited this long," Mayor Gribbins said, "and I don't
suppose another few days will hurt. We will, if all agree, give
you a week to decide on the matter. But then we must know.
We need law and order in Alamitos and if you haven't
decided in one week, someone else will be appointed."

"Fair enough," I said.

Standing up with everyone else, I shook hands all around

again, including a brief, grudging handshake from Watkins, and then I left the mayor's office. Lighting a cigar, I straddled Cap and sat for a minute wondering what to do next. The thought of a cold beer sent me to Harry's Place.

Along that ride I cussed myself out a good deal. It beat all how I could get myself in so many fixes without half trying. It wasn't like I was overly ambitious or liked butting into other folk's business. All I wanted was a small ranch and a few head of cattle . . . just a few acres I could call my own and might ride without the need of a tied-down gun.

That's all I wanted, but it seemed every time I turned around, trouble was nipping at my heels like a wolf after a buffalo.

When I got enough of the doldrums off to notice what was going on around me, it seemed the town was busier than usual. The streets were more crowded, the sounds of hustle and bustle louder, the air filled with the electricity of excitement and trouble.

When I pushed through the swinging doors of Harry's Place it was crowded too. More than two dozen rough, boisterous cowboys occupied the bar and most of the tables. Two bartenders shoved an endless supply of beer up and down the bar while a number of pretty but tired-looking girls delivered drinks to the tables and flirted with the cowboys.

Somehow Harry saw me come in and yelled at me. He was sitting with three other men at a table and waved until I saw him. I cut a zigzag through the crowd until I reached his table, found an empty chair, and sat down. Harry patted one of the pretty girls on the rear end as she walked past and asked her to bring a round of beers to the table. She grinned, swished her shapely bottom within an inch of Harry's face, and walked off.

She returned a minute later with a tray full of beer and sat one in front of each of us. When she bent over the table her breasts made a valiant effort to escape the low-cut dress she almost had on. "Anything else I can do for you, Harry?" she asked.

He smiled. "You know there is, darlin', but it'll have to wait till later."

She sighed. "Too bad."

We all watched her as she went back to work. "One of the advantages to owning a saloon," Harry said.

"I reckon," I said. "If you ever decide to take on a partner, look me up." Glancing around the saloon I saw that it was growing more crowded by the minute. "What's going on? This town is busier than a one-legged man in a kicking contest."

"Had two fair-sized herds come in," Harry said, "and more on the way. Normally we'd still be weeks away from the time when the big herds roll in, but we didn't have anything like a dry season this year.

"One of the trail drivers told me it's green and wet all the way from Texas to Arizona. And the herds coming in this early is going to mean extra money for Alamitos."

"Yes," I said, "and likely a lot of extra trouble to go along with it."

"True enough," Harry said. "Now, tell me about your meeting with our illustrious town council."

I briefly studied the three men sitting at the table with us. One was in his late forties or early fifties, dressed the way a reasonably well-to-do rancher dresses when he wants a night out on the town—brown suit cut western style, white shirt, string tie, new boots and Stetson.

The second man was only a bit younger, but dressed more like a working cowhand than like a man who could afford to hire his work done. He had a straight way of looking you in the eye that I took to.

The third man was young, not more than twenty, and looked much like any other cowboy except for his pistol. It was a short-barreled Colt, covered with fancy engraving and fitted with pearl grips. The holster and belt were black and liberally sprinkled with silver studs.

It was a fancy-Dan kind of rig, the kind that might draw laughter and challenges from the rougher element in town, but he wore it tied down for use and age doesn't mean much when it comes to killing. Still, he didn't seem to have the bearing of a man who'd used a gun for much except an occasional snake or a row of tin cans. But the truth was, I'd no real way of knowing.

Harry saw me looking the men over and quickly introduced them. The older man was Simon Kearns, owner of the *Flying K* ranch off to the north a piece. The middle-aged man was Bill Flynn, foreman of the ranch, and the young buck with the fancy pistol was Eddie Kearns, Simon's oldest son.

"They don't get in often," Harry said, "but you can count them on our side. Simon has had more than his share of rustling."

"The rustling is bad enough," Simon put in, "but two weeks ago some bastard ran a hundred head of my best stock off a cliff. Somebody's going to pay for that."

"And we all know who it should be," Eddie said. "Everybody knows Colby Ryan is the man behind all the robbery and rustling, but nobody is willing to do a damn thing about it."

"There's a lot of rustlers around," I said mildly. "Ryan can't be behind all of it."

"If he's the man behind it," Harry said, "he'll make a slip sooner or later."

"If it was up to me," Eddie said, "I'd go over to that saloon of his and ride him out of town on a rail."

"Easier said than done," I said. "Ryan may be a lot of things, but he's a tough man and he keeps himself surrounded by half a dozen gunmen night and day."

Eddie laughed. "I don't wear this gun for show. I'm as fast as anybody working for Ryan. Tell him, Bill."

Bill Flynn sipped his beer and stubbed out his cigar before speaking. "Yeah, you're fast. About as fast as any I've seen. But fast ain't everything. There's a world of difference between drawing down on a tin can and standing eyeball to eyeball with a man who can shoot back.

"Most of the time, fast don't mean much. What matters is being calm enough to put that first bullet where it will count, knowing all the while that the man you're facing has the same idea and might be a shade better at getting it done."

Eddie just sneered, but I knew then that I was right about his never using a gun against a man. Well, he'd learn . . . if he lived long enough.

Harry asked again about my meeting with the town council. I wasn't certain about letting it be known that Alamitos was now the county seat, but I hadn't been told it was a secret, and with Watkins in on it, it sure wouldn't be for long. I briefly explained what they had asked of me. Harry laughed. "It does beat all," he said, "how a peace-loving man like you keeps stepping in so much cow dung."

"I had pretty much the same thought while riding down here," I said. "I've pretty much reached the conclusion that it must have something to do with the company I keep."

Harry laughed. "That's worth the price of another beer," he said. "With all these thirsty cowboys coming up the trail, I guess I can afford to be generous."

"That'll be the day," I said. "But I'll take the beer."

Kearns took another one, too. He sipped and scowled. "I've always favored skinning my own skunks," he said. "Never had much use for a lawdog. But in this case, I wouldn't mind the help. It's getting so I'm hip-deep in skunks and plain don't have the time to skin them all. If you decide to take on the job, you can count on me for all the help I can give."

Another half dozen cowboys pushed through the door, whooping and yelling as they shoved a path to the bar. Even from where I sat I could hear their money jingling on the

bar as they paid for their drinks. Harry glanced at the bar
with a happy look slapped all over him. "I see what you
mean about the money," I said. "They sure seem free in
spending it."

"What else is it good for? Some of those cowboys have been
months on the trail, and it's a hard life. Oh, a few of them
will go easy and take most of their pay back with them, but
all most of them want is a chance to blow off steam. They
want whiskey and a willing woman and don't give a damn
what it costs.

"We'll never be as big as Abilene or Dodge City, but maybe
fifty herds will come through this year. Each herd will have
between twenty-five hundred and five thousand steers, and
one cowboy for each two hundred head. That's not counting
the trail boss, ramrod, cook, cook's helper, and two or three
men to handle the remuda. Throw in a couple of scouts for
good measure and that's a lot of men spending their pay
here.

"But that's nothing. It takes tons of money to buy the cattle
once they get here. That's where the real money is. A lot of
it comes in the form of bank drafts and the like, but some
folks want their due in cash, and they all need ready money
to pay off the drovers.

"Why, Chet Watkins bragged last year that his bank had
near two hundred thousand in *cash*."

I whistled. "That's money enough to tempt anyone," I
said. "I wonder some jasper didn't try to rob the bank."

"They did. Twice, in fact, but I'll give this to Watkins,
nobody ever got away from his bank with a penny. He always
hires three or four men this time of year, and he arms them
with sawed-off Greeners. A couple of the would-be holdup
men looked like sieves, and only one managed to live long
enough to reach the jail before cashing in his chips at the
end of a rope."

"That's still an awful lot of money. It may be safe in the
bank, but what about after it's paid out and the herd owners

are on the trail back home? Seems to me it would be pretty easy to waylay a stage or a couple of tired men and grab some easy money."

Harry nodded. "It happens a few times evey year. Darndest thing, too. Every time some poor bastard gets robbed, Colby Ryan seems to get a little richer."

"There may be a lot of money in the bank this time of year," Kearns said, "but none of it's mine. I keep enough on hand for my needs and the rest is in a bank over to Santa Fe."

"Santa Fe?" Harry said. "Hell, that's over a hundred miles! What happens if you need money sudden like?"

"That's what they invented the telegraph for," he said. "Truth is, there's something about Chet Watkins that I don't take to. For one thing, he takes too much interest in Colby Ryan's money."

"I reckon money is money to a banker," I said, "but I can see your point."

"So, not to change the subject," Harry said, "but are you going to be our new county sheriff, or aren't you?"

"I honestly don't know," I said. "I really do want to think about it for a spell. I wish I knew a little more about Colby Ryan before I decide, like just who the men are he trusts and which ones stick the closest to him."

"How would that help?" Flynn asked. "In either case you'll either have to handle them or backwater."

"True enough," I said, "but knowing the kind of men they are and how they operate might give me a better idea of *how* to handle them. Some men you can handle easier from behind a badge, but others you can't.

"Sometimes with hired killers or backshooters it's easier to leave the badge off and meet them on their own ground. With a star pinned to your shirt you're held to certain rules the other guy doesn't have to follow."

"It makes sense," Harry said, "but the only way to do it is to see for yourself. I could name all the men around Ryan, but unless you watched them, felt them out for yourself, it wouldn't mean much. It's a shame you can't spend a few hours sitting in the Silver Slipper. That might give you all the information you need."

I drank the last of my beer and smiled at Harry. "Now that is what I call an idea," I said. "I wonder I didn't think of it myself."

Harry's jaw dropped open. "I was just funnin'," he said. "You don't really intend to go in there, do you?"

"Why not?"

"Because Ryan would like as not have one of his men put a bullet in your back before you left, is why!"

"I doubt it. Oh, another time, maybe, but not now. Look, the herds are starting to come in, right? Well, you're getting a lot of business from them, but every man I've seen through those swinging doors is a drover . . . thirty a month and found.

"Now, where are the trail bosses and herd owners you spoke of? They get thirsty, too, don't they?"

"Sure, and you know where they are. Men with that kind of money go to the Silver Slipper."

"That's right, and Ryan counts on them for a good bit of his honest income. And some of them are certainly loose-lipped enough to drop information Ryan can use. No, he isn't going to risk driving them away because I come in for a drink or two. He won't like it, but he won't bother me."

"Seems to me that's pretty chancy guessing," Harry said, "but you do have a point. But what's to stop him from following you when you leave and putting a bullet in your back?"

"Hell, he'll try that sooner or later anyway, but I think he may let it go. I'm just a worrisome thorn right now. Probably not even worth bothering about with all this easy money floating around."

"So you're really going to do it," Harry said. "When?"

I stood up and shoved away from the table. "Right now is as good a time as any. I'll see you around."

I took about two steps before Harry stooped me. "Just hold on a danged minute," he said. I stopped and he stood up and walked to the bar. He went behind the bar and took a holstered Colt from a shelf, flipped the belt around his waist and fastened it in place, then tied the holster to his leg.

That done he spoke a minute to one of the bartenders and walked back to me. "Let's go," he said.

I laughed. "I thought you said it was foolish. What made you want to go with me?"

"It is foolish, but I guess I'm as big a damn fool as you. I'd like to see Ryan's face when we come through the door. Might be worth getting shot at."

"It might, at that," I said, "so long as we don't get *hit*."

We went out the door and I straddled my horse. Harry walked to a livery a block away and saddled one of his own, then we set off for the Silver Slipper.

CHAPTER 8

WE cut over a couple of streets, skirting the edge of town to avoid the boisterous cowboys thronging the main drags. The day was in the final stages of death, and the western sky was pulling down a beautiful purple and crimson final curtain.

It was quieter where we rode, though a distant buzz of activity from Alamitos still came to us. Harry opened his mouth to say something, then paused, a sudden attentive look on his face. "Did you hear something?" he asked. "Out there on the prairie?"

I had, but really hadn't paid it any mind. I wasn't sure, but the sound may have been gunshots far enough away to be barely in the range of hearing. "You tell me," I said.

"A Colt, I think. Three quick shots, half a mile or so out?"

The sounds came again, and this time we were paying attention. No doubt about it, someone was firing a pistol. Again they fired three times, then silence. "What do you make of it," I asked. "Think it might be trouble?"

Harry sighed. "Three shots, then silence, then three more shots? Yeah, I expect it's trouble. I also expect you'll want to ride out and see what's happening for yourself."

"You read my mind," I said. "Let's go."

Harry smiled. "I got a feeling," he said, "that hitching my horse to your wagon ain't the smartest thing I ever did."

That's what he said, but he followed me out onto the prairie. We rode slowly, the thongs off our Colts and ready for anything. A full moon was climbing the night sky, and the visibility was good. Too good, in fact. Riding high in the saddle on a night like that, you could be picked off easily by anybody within a hundred yards.

After a spell we heard the shots again, and again there were three of them, silence, then three more. We were obviously much closer to the source now, and the shots were loud and clear, the thunder of them rolling over the land and coming to us from the southwest. We slowed even more.

When the next shots came I saw the flame spurt into the air only a few hundred yards away. "No doubt about it," Harry said, "That's a man in trouble."

"Maybe, but let's go in slow. He may be in trouble, or he may just be waiting to start it."

At something less than a hundred yards the man must have seen us, tall against the night sky as we were, but all I could make out of him was a dark blob against the grass. Anyway, he called out to us, a weak, shaky voice that carried the distance between us but brought no meaning with it.

"He's hurt," I said. "Bad, by the sound of it. Lay back a little and cover me. I'm going in."

At fifty yards Harry pulled up and shucked his rifle from the scabbard. "I don't guarantee I can hit anything by the light of the moon," he said, "but you get in trouble and I'll dust things up enough to give you a chance."

I nodded and started toward the man on the grass. There was no sound from him, no sound from anywhere except the soft step of Cap in the tall grass and the shallow whisper of my own breathing. At thirty yards I got down off Cap and walked forward.

At twenty feet I stopped. The man was half sitting, half laying on the grass, his back against a boulder. A Colt lay next to his hand and his eyes were closed. I called out, asking him who he was. His eyes snapped open, and when he saw me he tried to grab the Colt. It slipped from his hand and he let it lay.

Taking a chance, I moved up to him and knelt down. His shirt and pants were soaked with blood, but he was still breathing. I opened his shirt carefully and saw three holes in his belly, all made by a large-caliber gun. I bandaged him as best I could. I'd seen such wounds a time or two before and it was a miracle he was alive.

I waved to Harry. When he approached I explained what I'd found. "He hasn't a chance," I said, "but you better ride for Doc Priter."

Harry rode off, going back to town at a gallop, and I built a small fire from the sticks and dry grass laying about. In the light of the fire the man looked older than I'd first thought. His clothing was bloodstained and dirty but obviously new and expensive. While I was looking at his boots he opened his eyes.

"First store-bought boots I ever owned," he said softly. "I never wanted to die with my boots on, but then again, I never owned boots like these. Reckon they'll do to bury me in."

"What happened out here? Who are you?" I asked, dabbing his forehead with a damp kerchief.

"Name's Evan Cory," he said. "I brought a small herd up from Texas and sold 'em in Alamitos. Got near twenty thousand in gold for just under a thousand head of cattle that I couldn't give away a few years ago.

"Funny, I never had much in my life, and never missed it either. Now I make enough to see me through the last years in some kind of comfort, and I get shot. Hell of a note."

"Who shot you?"

He shrugged a little, coughed, and moaned in pain at the effort. "Don't know who they were, but they sure knew what they wanted. I left Alamitos an hour or so before dark, figuring maybe if anybody was waiting to rob me, the hour might throw them off a bit.

"I should've known better. First I knew anyone was around was when a rifle bullet took my horse out from under me. I went down hard, and hadn't more than got to my feet when a second bullet took me square in the belly. Knocked me down, but it surprised me more than anything. Anyway, three men came riding from out of nowhere and went about going through my saddlebags like I wasn't even there. My pistol got lost somewhere in the fall my horse took, and all I could do was lay there and watch.

"They took my gold and got back in the saddle. Then one, a big fellow with something odd about his nose, pulled a pistol and shot me twice more in the belly. I must have passed out, and I reckon they left me for dead."

It was a common enough story. A lot of men rode out with gold and were never seen again. Still, it rankled. Evan Cory sized up as a good man, and a hardworking one. All he'd wanted was enough money to see him through the hard years ahead, and he had earned it.

It's no easy job for a young man to drive a herd of wild Texas cattle through desert heat and raging rivers. For a man the age of Evan Cory, it took a lot of guts.

"I got to ask you," I said. "Is there anyone I should write, a family or the like?"

"No. I had a wife and a son once, but they both drowned in a flash flood. It just wasn't in me to marry again after that. I paid off my hands back in Alamitos, but there's no reason any of them should care what happens to me. I didn't know any of them before the drive. I got a favor to ask you, though, if you're of a mind."

"Name it."

"If you happen to run across a big man with a funny nose, and if he happens to be spending gold like it was easy come, put a bullet in him for me."

"You can count on it."

He leaned back and closed his eyes. A minute later I saw Doc Priter's buggy come racing across the grass, Harry riding alongside. They were too late. Evan Cory was dead.

We loaded his body into Doc Priter's buggy so he could be taken back to Alamitos for proper burial, but Harry and I didn't ride back with the doc. I doubted it would do much good, but I wanted to look around.

"You any good at tracking?" I asked Harry.

"My pa used to say I could track a wet frog across a lily pond," he said. "But he was stretching things a little."

I laughed. "Think you can track well enough by moonlight to tell which way the men who shot Cory went?"

"I can try."

It seemed an impossible task I was giving him, but he took to it like a duck to water. With the moonlight and a handful of matches, Harry studied the ground. Then he swung a wide circle on foot. I could see him off in the darkness as he occasionally bent and struck a match. He then backtracked the trail of the men who killed Cory.

Harry was better at tracking than I'd ever be, so I sat astride Cap and waited for him to finish. When he returned, he climbed back aboard his horse and sat quietly for several minutes, apparently lost in thought. "There were four men, not three," he said at last. "One of them sat on that knoll yonder and watched the whole thing. I figure him for the boss."

"What else? Anything to say who they were?"

"About the boss, no. But let me show you something."

He slipped from the saddle again and I went with him. Just a few yards from where Evan Cory was shot, Harry knelt and struck a match, cupping it from the breeze with his hands. The light of the match revealed the sharp print of a horseshoe . . . a shoe with a star-shaped nick in it.

I swore softly, then told Harry about finding a similar track at Lysander's ranch.

"Looks like a fellow who gets around a good bit," Harry said. "I wonder where he'll turn up next?"

"Wherever it is, he shouldn't be hard to find."

"Not if he stays around Alamitos," Harry said. "By the sharpness of the track, I'd say that was a new shoe, so it'll be at least a month before he needs the job done again."

"Any idea which way they went?"

"Back to Alamitos by the look of it. And it'd take more luck than I have to track them there. Too many horses and the like muddling things up. We might try the stables, but it isn't likely the horse will be there. These gents are too clever for that, and they aren't strangers."

"What makes you say that?"

"Just a feeling, mostly. A man rides different in strange country. The trail is generally straighter and seldom follows the easiest path. This trail takes the easiest way, and makes use of every speck of cover. No, at least one of the men in this crowd has been around a good while. If it's true of one of them, then likely it's true of them all."

It made sense, but damn it, I wanted this bunch. But bad as I wanted them, it would have to wait for another day. I said as much to Harry.

"It galls me too," he said. "And you haven't seen the worst of it.

"That bloody splotch on the grass over there is where Cory was laying when he was shot twice more. You said Cory told you the man who did it was big and had a funny nose—well, now we know he also rides a horse with a nick in the left front shoe."

"You sure that's the right track?"

"Line it up. The other two horses never get in front of this one. I'd stake my life on it."

"If it's true, then sooner or later I'll find him."

"Be careful when you do," Harry said. "Whoever he is, he's as cold-blooded a killer as I've ever seen."

We started back for Alamitos then, riding slow and lost in thought. It was more than an honest man like Cory being killed that bothered me, it was how anyone knew he was carrying gold. Most of the cattle buyers and herd owners dealt with bank drafts, only using cash to pay off their trail hands and the like.

"How would someone know who was carrying cash?" I asked Harry. "Something smells about all these holdups."

"Likely a loose mouth," Harry said. "A man gets a pocketful of money and he gets the urge to talk."

"Maybe, but it's happening too often. Evan Cory struck me as a closemouthed man where money came in. I guess what I'm asking is, who would know if the man didn't talk about it?"

Harry thought a minute. "Well, the bank would know. That adds up to three or four people right there. And who knows who might be in the bank when a herd owner or the like was doing business. What are you trying to get at, anyway?"

"Nothing, maybe. Then again, maybe it's everything. Just seems to me that whoever is pulling these holdups knows more than they should. If we could learn where they're getting their information it might help."

"It might, but how do you go about finding out? I can track and read sign with the best of them, but mysteries are out of my line."

"How much do you know about Chet Watkins?"

"Not much, when you get down to it. Watkins isn't what I'd call a sociable man."

"I'm grasping at straws, I guess. Thing is, I can see where the bank might be prosperous now, but how did Watkins pull through the lean years before the cattle trade built to where it is now?"

"I couldn't begin to tell you," Harry said. "But now that you mention it, it does seem that he had a bit more money to spread around than the few depositors around Alamitos could account for. I'll tell you this, when Colby Ryan turned up in Alamitos he didn't have enough money to buy a train ticket back out, but Watkins did business with him anyway. Gave him loans and the like to get started."

"Maybe he thought it was a good gamble. Did Ryan have anything at all for collateral?"

"Not where it could be seen."

We rode on in silence for a while, and I used the time to go over things in my mind. The facts were few: Colby Ryan was slowly absorbing as many ranches as possible. Rustling was wide spread and growing more so with each passing day. Ryan had acquired at least a couple of his holdings under dubious circumstances.

Throw in the fact that the local banker had given Ryan loans when he should have turned him down cold, and what did you have?

Nothing, damn it. Not one damn thing other than suspicions that Ryan was anything other than an honest businessman.

There was no law against buying more and more land. Or employing gunhands, unless they were already wanted by the law for crimes of their own. Time too was on Ryan's side. After a while he would reach the point where he no longer needed to rustle or steal or murder to gain ground.

Of course, I had no idea how much money Ryan had, or how much he had to put out to maintain his holdings, but the thing I was counting on was greed.

Ryan already owned enough of the pie to satisfy most men, but he struck me as the kind who would want all the slices for himself. If I read him right, he would push and shove, spending all the money necessary, robbing and killing when he needed more, until the pie was all his. Then he'd go looking for another pie.

But the fact remained that unless he made a mistake, or unless we got a break somewhere along the line, we might not be able to stop him.

What we needed was to catch some of the rustlers in the act. Put enough pressure on them, or around their necks, and they might implicate Ryan. As my pa used to say, most any man will spill his guts to save his neck, and that looked to be the best shot we had at Ryan.

But even that was far from an easy shot. New Mexico was wild and wide, mostly uninhabited, and it bordered Mexico. Once across that border, any rustled cattle were out of reach. But what I had to believe was that Ryan was human and prone to the same mistakes and plain, out-and-out bad luck that befell any other man.

But whether it came down to a mistake by Ryan, or just a case of bad luck, he had to be stopped. No man had the right to further himself at the expense of innocent people who wanted nothing more than a chance to build a home and family in peace.

For the sake of men like John Lysander and Evan Cory, Colby Ryan had to be stopped.

Harry broke the silence. "You still intend to visit the Silver Slipper tonight?"

"More than ever. If I'm to stop Ryan from riding up my front and down my backside, I need to know the faces of the men working for him. I'm not looking forward to it, but somehow I need to rattle Ryan, even if it's nothing more than being there when he turns around. If I can make him nervous, make him hurry things, then maybe he'll slip."

"Maybe, but it's a dangerous game. Truth is, I doubt you have to worry about rattling him. The one thing he can't tolerate is a man with your reputation turning down his offer of a job, then going to work for the other side.

"He's got to knock you down hard and fast to save face, and to keep any other would-be opposition from taking a stand. If he can stop you, others might be afraid to try."

We came back into Alamitos still talking, and I turned Cap down the street toward the Silver Slipper. I'd no doubt that Harry had the situation pegged down solid, but there was little choice in the matter. If I let Ryan make all the moves the game might be over before I had a chance to play.

"You ready to go visiting?" I asked Harry.

"Why not? He can kill us, but he can't eat us . . . that's against the law."

CHAPTER 9

WE tied our horses at a hitch rail just down the street from the Silver Slipper and walked slowly to the door. We stopped outside for a minute and gave the place the once-over. It was full of people, maybe three or four times as many as Harry's could even hold, and all of them, men and women alike, dressed a sight better than we were.

"It isn't too late to turn around and go back the way we came," Harry said. "I'm not afraid of Ryan, but mixing in with a crowd like this just plain gives me the jitters."

Truth was, it did me too. "We've come this far," I said, "and I'm a man who likes to get where he started for. Let's go on in and find a table."

"Yeah, one where we can keep our backs to the wall."

We went through the door and edged through the crowd, aiming at a free table in a far corner. Most of the folks took no notice of us, but here and there some lady would wrinkle up her nose and back away.

We reached the table and sat down, our backs to the wall as Harry had suggested. We were both jumpy, feeling out of place, and I had a nervous itch down the middle of my back—the kind you get when someone has rifle sights trained on you. But if we expected to raise a ruckus, we were sadly disappointed. A number of folks about the place were watching us, but other than that, we may as well have stayed home.

"Maybe they're afraid of us," Harry said. "Not a soul coming near."

I laughed. "I doubt that's it. I don't see Ryan around anywhere and they probably don't want to move without him."

Whatever the reason, we were being ignored and that was fine by me. All I wanted was a chance to look around and get the feel of Ryan's world. Sitting in a chair, being left alone, was the perfect opportunity to do just that.

"You wanted to know who Ryan keeps around him on a regular basis," Harry said. "Well, most of them are here right now, and we seem to be the center of attention with them."

Harry started pointing out men for me. Four of them were made in the same mold, and Harry named them first. "The two at the table by the door are Jack Strayer and Dan Ames, the one in the doorway over there is Dale Mobley and up yonder on the staircase is Paul Cole.

"They're all hired guns, about average in their field. But put two or three of them together and they make a package."

Two men came out of nowhere and sat down at a table not far from us. The look on their faces wasn't friendly. "Uh-huh," Harry said. "Now we're getting somewhere. Those two near live inside Ryan's long johns. The big gent is Frank Heart. He can use a gun if need be, but breaking bones is what he does best.

"The skinny weasel is Leon Pratt. Leon is a knife man, in the back whenever possible. They say he can throw that knife of his better than most men can use a pistol."

"You know," I said. "Strayer is a big man, and that broken nose might look odd in the dim light. I'd like to get a look at his horse."

"Now that's a thought," Harry said.

These six were only a few of Ryan's hired guns, but they were the first line, and they'd be plenty to handle. Ryan obviously wanted enough men around to discourage anyone from picking a fight with him. These boys might be thugs and hired killers, but they were still fighting men of the first order.

Colby Ryan came out then and made straight for us. There was no hint of surprise on his face, and I knew he'd been warned before coming out. And I'll give him this—he didn't seem any put out about us being there. In fact, he had a smile on his face that made me want to check my hole card.

He stopped at our table and smiled even wider. "It's a real pleasure seeing you boys," he said. "I'm glad you dropped in. Is there something in particular you want?"

"Just stopped in for a drink," I said, "and a chance to see how the other half lives."

"Fine," Ryan said, "just fine. And you, Mr. Morgan, what brings you here?"

"Oh, just thought it might be a wise idea to check on my competition. Good business practice, or so they tell me."

"It is, at that," Ryan said. "In fact, I think it might be a good idea for me to pay a visit to your establishment one day soon. Might be I'd learn something."

"I can guarantee that," Harry said.

"Then I'll make a note to do just that." He held a hand up and made a small gesture. When he did one of the bartenders came running. "Make these gentlemen comfortable," Ryan said. "Anything they ask for is on the house."

He turned back to us. "What will it be? Steak, beer?"

It was Harry's turn to smile. "I'm not really hungry," he said, "but I will have something to drink. I've never tasted champagne, but I've always had a hankering to. And I understand you have some of the finest anywhere."

Harry turned to the bartender. "Suppose you do like Mr. Ryan says and get us a bottle, the best you have. On the house."

Ryan's face was a shade whiter than before, but when the bartender looked at him he nodded. "Enjoy it while you can," he said. "It costs somewhere around twenty dollars a bottle."

That made me turn a shade whiter, but Harry took it in stride.

"What's a few dollars between friends," he said. "Next time I'll pay."

"Of that you can be certain," Ryan said. "Now, if you will excuse me, I have business to attend to."

He walked away and I let out a breath I didn't know I'd been holding. "For a man who thought it was foolish to come here," I said to Harry, "you sure take chances."

"Guess I did get a little carried away, but you know what? I have always had a hankering for champagne."

We sat there and jawed the fat for near twenty minutes and still no champagne. I was about to think that Ryan had changed his mind when this fellow dressed in a waiter's outfit pushed a cart to our table. On the cart was a bucket of ice, and in the ice a bottle of wine.

The fellow opened the bottle and the cork flew about ten feet. Then he pour a tiny little dribble in two glasses and gave them to us. "I think we're supposed to taste it," Harry said.

I picked the glass up and took a sip, then Harry did the same thing. It bubbled up funny and kind of tickled on the way down, but it wasn't bad. Harry grinned. "Just like I thought it would be," he said. "I was afraid I wouldn't like it."

"It's pretty good at that," I said. I looked at the waiter. "Fill 'em up and then stand aside."

He sniffed like maybe he smelled something he didn't like, but he did as he was told without a word. I took a long pull on that full glass and it went down smooth as buttermilk. Then, from the corner of my eye, I saw a man approaching our table. I turned to get a better look. He was young, dressed even better than Ryan had been, and he was undoubtably the handsomest man I'd ever seen. He sized up like a rich cattle buyer or the like, but then I saw his eyes.

They were blue and cold, but there was something else about them that I couldn't really put a finger on . . . something disturbing. He came right to us and tipped his hat. "You are, I believe, James Darnell," he said. "May I join you?"

"I am James Darnell," I said, "but do I know you?"

"Probably in the same way I know you," the man said. "My name is Con Ferris."

I flinched and Harry almost choked on his champagne. "It seems I have heard the name somewhere," I said. "I believe you're said to be pretty good with a six-gun."

"So they say."

"Well," I said, "it's a pleasure to meet you. Sit down and join us. Have a glass of champagne. There's plenty to go around."

He sat down. "Thank you, I believe I will."

I got another glass from the waiter and filled it, then handed it to Ferris. He sipped it delicately. "Excellent," he said. "I'm surprised a cowboy could afford it. You must have struck gold somewhere."

"Colby Ryan bought it," I said. "I believe he hopes it's a going-away present, so to speak."

"Whatever his reason, it's well worth it."

Harry hadn't said a word the whole time and didn't look as if he wanted to. He kept flicking his eyes back and forth between Ferris and me like he couldn't believe what was happening.

"Tell me, Mr. Ferris," I said. "What brings you to Alamitos? It is a little off the beaten path."

"You know how it is in this line of work," he said. "The pay is good, but you have to go where the business is."

That Con Ferris was in Alamitos *might* have been coincidence; that he came to our table could not be. "That's true enough," I said, "But I believe you should reconsider working here. The air isn't at all healthy."

"Really? What's wrong with it?"

"It's full of lead and getting worse by the day," I said. "Yes, sir, a man could catch his death here."

"I thought the air was a bit thick," he said. "However, I seem to have built up an immunity in my travels, so I think I'll be all right. How about you, Mr. Darnell?"

I smiled. "I feel fine," I said.

"That's good to hear. Now, while it has been pleasant, I really shouldn't impose on you any longer. I do thank you for the champagne. Everyone should taste it once before they die."

"We've both had our taste," I said, "in case either of us should be unlucky enough to die soon."

He stood up. "True enough. Until we meet again, Mr. Darnell, and I have no doubt we will."

"I'm sure of it," I said.

He nodded and walked off. It was only then I realized what was odd about his eyes. They were flat like a snake's and didn't show any trace of emotion. I had a feeling Con Ferris was by far the most dangerous man I'd ever met.

When he was gone Harry killed his glass of champagne in one gulp. "Sweet mother of God," he said. "What was that all about?"

I lit a cigar and rolled it around my lips. "It would seem Colby Ryan has a new man working for him," I said. "And unless I miss my guess, he's been hired to kill me."

"I never would have believed it," he said. "Con Ferris in Alamitos. James, my boy, you better check you hole card. If even half of the stories told about him are true, then you best settle your debts and make your will."

"I was on a trail drive with a man one time," I said. "Folks said he was faster than Billy the Kid and Will Bill Hickock put together, and a dead shot to boot."

"What happened to him?"

"He picked a fight with one of the drovers, a Mexican not even ready to shave yet. That Mexican kid shot him four times before he even cleared leather. We buried him right there on the spot."

"Huh," Harry grunted. "I'll take your word for that, but if it's all the same to you, I won't be loaning you any money for a spell, and you pay for your food and drinks in advance."

I laughed. "Fair enough. Now I think it's time we got out of here before we wear out our welcome."

"Amen," Harry said.

We went out quick and walked down the street to our horses. Once in the saddle we started away from the Silver Slipper at a fast walk. Just as we reached the corner I decided to light a cigar. It was a decision that saved my life.

I stuck the end of the cigar in my mouth, struck a match and bent my head down to touch match to cigar. As I dipped my head something tugged hard at my hat. Almost at the same time I heard the roar of a rifle. I dove from the saddle and landed face down in the mud behind a watering trough, Harry landing beside me.

We both had our Colts out, and I slowly peeked over the edge of the trough. The street was already filling with people, curious as to who was shooting at what. Whoever had fired the shot was long gone.

We stood up, wet, muddy, and miserable, and Harry cussed a blue streak for about ten minutes, most of it aimed at me. My cigar was a sodden mess and I threw it away. "That was way too close," I said, "but I guess an inch is as good as a mile."

"An inch is right," Harry said. "Take a look at your hat."

I removed my hat and held it up toward a street lamp in order to see it better. What I saw made me shiver. There was a bullet hole through the crown, and I had no idea how the bullet had missed my head. If I hadn't bent to light that cigar somebody would have saved Con Ferris a lot of trouble.

We got back in the saddle and rode to Harry's place, then I went off toward Zeb's ranch. I'd had enough of Alamitos for one day . . . or for one lifetime.

CHAPTER 10

IT was pretty near ten at night when I rode into sight of Zeb's ranch, but even at that I could still see a light in the window. Then I caught the smell of wood smoke, followed immediately by the aroma of hot food. I hadn't really eaten since morning, and my stomach was letting me know about it.

I was hungry, but I took the time to stable my horse in the barn, giving him a good rubdown and a bucket of grain. Then I slung my saddle over a sawhorse and walked to the house. Zeb was standing in the shadows near the porch, a .50-caliber buffalo gun clutched in his right hand. "Heard the horse coming," he said. "Wasn't sure it was you."

We went into the house, and the warmth folded around me like a welcome hug. I didn't even slow down, but headed straight for the kitchen. Mary Kay was way ahead of me, already setting a platter of cornbread, a pot of beans, and half a dozen pieces of fried chicken on the table. She put me out a plate and set a large cup of black coffee next to it. "I thought it was probably you dragging in late," she said. "I never knew a man who wasn't hungry at the end of a long day."

"I might have eaten in town."

"You might have, but you aren't that smart."

Matching wits with Mary Kay looked like a losing proposition, so I quickly changed the subject. "How's John?"

"Better, I think. He stirred around a couple of hours ago and tried to open his eyes."

"That is good news. Doc Priter said he'd be out tomorrow."

"I'm glad to hear that," Mary Kay said. "I was considering changing John's bandages myself."

"Has Nolan been around? I kept expecting him to drift into town, but he never showed."

"He hasn't been here. Do you think he might be in trouble?"

"Anybody tackles Nolan, they're the ones in trouble. No, he's likely too far out to get back in tonight." Outside there came a crash of thunder and rain started pelting the roof. "Of course," I added, "he might be a little wet."

Zeb came in and poured himself a cup of coffee before sitting down. He watched me put away food like my leg was hollow, and there was no humor on his face. "I'd rather pay you fighting wages than feed you," he said. "I never saw a man who could put away grub like you do."

"You know," I said, "my pa used to complain about that from time to time. He said that when I left home two farmers, a rancher, and at least three grain mills would have to close down."

"I reckon he wasn't too far wrong, either," Zeb said. "Well, I'm going to check on John and then turn in. These old bones of mine start complaining if I stay up too late. You younguns have fun."

Zeb stood up and stretched, then went off to bed. Mary Kay refilled my coffee cup, poured herself a cup, and sat down across from me. She seemed prettier every time I saw her, and she still had that look in her eye, but somehow it didn't bother me near as much as it had the first time I saw it. That bothered me in itself.

It wasn't that I didn't like her, or more than like her, and it wasn't that I wanted to spend my days walking alone, but I had nothing to offer. If anything, every day that passed left me with less.

No, when and if I married I wanted to be able to look out on land I could call my own. I wanted a comfortable home where I could raise a family, and I wanted enough money in my pocket to give my wife the frills and doodads that women seem to place such store by.

Not that Mary Kay would have me anyway, in spite of that look in her eyes. In most ways women seem to be a lot more sensible than men, and Mary Kay was no fool. She could certainly do better than a wandering cowboy who owned only what he wore on his back or had stashed in his saddlebags.

She was quite a woman any way you looked at her . . . or listened to her, for that matter. She had a way of speaking that was better than the average person and I asked her about it. She shrugged. "I spent four years at a fancy college back East. I enjoyed it, and I'm happy I went through it, but after four years I couldn't wait to get back home."

"I know what you mean," I said. "I was in Chicago once, rode a cattle car there for a man who sold a herd of cattle. Never saw so much I could live without."

"Washington, now," Mary Kay said. "That is another story. It was the most beautiful city you can imagine. I'd like to go back there one day. You really should see it."

"I'd like that. Tell me, how come you didn't latch onto one of those Eastern fellows? Seems to me they'd have been beating your door down."

"Not so you would notice. The men seemed to find me . . . well, intimidating. At least that's the way one of them put it."

I smiled at her. "Intimidating? You are the most beautiful woman I've ever seen, and on top of that you're intelligent and quick-witted. You hold your head up and look a man in the eye when you speak to him, and you don't take sass from anyone. You're also more of a lady than anyone I've ever met.

"But intimidating? No, ma'am. Challenging might be a word I'd use, but not intimidating."

Mary Kay's face was flushed, and there was a brightness in her eyes that should have frightened me, but didn't. "So," she said, "you think I'm a challenge? Does that mean you aren't going to come courting after all?"

I sipped my coffee, looked at her, and grinned. "I thought

you knew me better than that," I said. "There's nothing I like better than a challenge."

"I'm glad to hear that," she said. "And I'll hold you to it."

We talked for the better part of two more hours before turning in, and even after that I stayed awake quite a spell, staring at the ceiling and thinking of Mary Kay and my future. In spite of my loose talk, she was way out of my class, and well I knew it.

It wasn't just her beauty and the fact that she was such a lady. It was also that she was not only intelligent, but had the education to go with it. She'd had four years of college, and I hadn't had any more schooling than the average ten-year-old. Oh, I could make my way through a book, but when the talk turned to poetry or the like, I was flat lost.

And the truth of the matter was, I just couldn't see any reason why a woman as beautiful as Mary Kay would have anything to do with a big, homely country boy like me anyway.

It seemed all I had ahead was a lonely stretch of years and the likelihood of always working for someone else until I was too old to do more than sit in the sun and think about what might have been. I wanted a ranch of my own, but it just wasn't all that easy.

If hard work alone could turn the trick I had nothing to worry about, but hard work alone wasn't enough. I'd seen men work eighteen hours a day, doing everything right, and still fail miserably. Building a ranch took money, but it also took more than a little luck. All it took to ruin years of work was one blizzard, a drought, or a rampant case of anthrax.

I'd never had much in the way of luck, and it wasn't something I could even begin to count on. Maybe a few years down the road, when and if I ever made something of myself, maybe then I could think about Mary Kay. But not now.

Somewhere in the middle of these thoughts I fell off to sleep.

CHAPTER 11

IT was a rooster, sitting on a fence post in the predawn light, that woke me from a sound sleep. I closed my eyes and tried to doze off again, but that rooster would have none of it. He let out another cock-a-doodle-doo, announcing to the world that another day was here and he was still the king.

I'd half a mind to grab my pistol and have rooster stew for breakfast, but sat up instead and scratched the stubble of beard on my face. By the time I came fully awake I realized there was an unpleasant odor in the room. It took only a couple of sniffs to find the source—me!

Dressing quickly, I went into the kitchen. Someone was stirring in a back room, but so far I was the only one out and about. I dug a towel from a drawer in the kitchen and a bar of soap from beside the washbasin outside the door, then wandered down to a fast-moving stream a hundred yards from the house.

It wasn't much of a stream, not over ten feet wide, but all I needed was enough water to get the dirt off. Stripping down to the buff, I jumped in before I could change my mind. When I hit that water I screamed and bounced all the way back to the bank with one hop.

Now, I expected that water to be cold, but I've been in blizzards that were warmer than that little stream. I stood on the bank and shivered for a minute, then broke the icicles off various portions of my anatomy and waded back in, figuring I needed a bath enough to risk pneumonia.

I sure enough needed a bath though, cause once I started scrubbing with that cake of soap, two frogs went belly up and a pair of muskrats jumped out of the water and took off for the woods.

After scrubbing for a spell, a *short* spell, I got out of the water, toweled down, and dressed in record time. What I wanted more than anything else was to get inside the house and melt the ice off my skin, but I stopped outside and shaved first, staring into a fragment of mirror hanging from the side of the house.

Thinking a mustache couldn't hurt my looks any, I left that and went inside, still shivering, to find Mary Kay awake and at it in the kitchen. She had the fire already going and was fixing breakfast, but food could wait. I huddled next to the cookstove, near hugging it, and refused to move until I was warm.

Mary Kay laughed till she was red in the face. "If you'd waited till I was awake," she said, "I could have saved you some grief. We have a tub in the bedroom, and it would have taken only a few minutes to heat some water."

"N-n-now you tell me," I said.

"I'm glad I didn't tell you sooner. Blue is definitely your color."

I'd have hit her, but she was too far from the stove and I wasn't about to move.

Zeb came into the kitchen, yawning and looking like an old bear just out of hibernation. "Good news," he said. "John came out of it for a minute, long enough to ask what happened. He dropped back off, but it's just sleep this time. He's going to be fine, if you ask me."

"I'm mighty glad to hear that," I said. "Doc Priter will be here this morning. He should know by now how it's going to be for John."

Mary Kay had a pot of coffee going and I was still cold. Grabbing a cup, I filled it, drank it down without waiting for it to cool much, then tried for a refill. Mary Kay hit me with a wooden spoon. "If you aren't warm by now," she said, "you never will be. Now get away from the stove and let me fix some breakfast."

I refilled the cup and moved before she could hit me again, sitting down at the table with Zeb. He winked at me and went for his own cup of coffee. He poured a cup and expertly ducked a wild swing of the spoon without spilling a drop. "You did that real well," I said when he sat down. "My arm still stings."

"Just takes practice," he said. "Stick around and you'll get the hang of it."

Mary Kay grunted and gave Zeb a look that might have killed a lesser man, but she let it go at that and went on with making breakfast. In a few minutes' time she had eggs and bacon frying and a large pan of biscuits in the oven. Time it was done my stomach was throwing a fit to get at it. Mary Kay set out a bowl of homemade butter to top the biscuits with, and we all dug in.

Zeb and Mary Kay got off to a pretty good start, but they finished slow. When they'd both shoved away from the table with a full belly, three eggs, half a dozen strips of bacon, and two biscuits remained unclaimed.

Me, I never was one to waste food . . . seemed unnatural, somehow, so I scooped all that was left into my plate and made short work of it. I poured another cup of coffee to wash everything down, leaned back, and lit a cigar. "That was real fine," I said. "What time is lunch?"

Zeb's jaw dropped and Mary Kay shook her head, but before either of them could reply the door opened and Nolan Blocke stepped in. He was dirty, unshaven, and looked fit to chew nails.

"Thought I smelled food," he said, "but it looks like I'm a mite late."

"Won't take a minute to cook more," Mary Kay said, "but if I were you I'd keep between James and the stove. He's like as not to take the food right out of the skillet."

Nolan took off his gunbelt, washed up a bit, and sat down at the table. "Feels good to be under a roof again," he said.

"I'd just about given you up for lost," I said. "Looked for you back last night."

"Would have been, but I had to do some tracking and all the rain we had slowed me down some."

"You look like you covered some territory."

"I did that," he said. "Went over most of John's south range. Found what I was looking for, too. I knew we were missing some cattle and once I got determined enough, I found out why.

"First thing I noticed was a cattle trail. Just a small group, half a dozen head or so. They were traveling along at a good clip and obviously being pushed, but there wasn't hide nor hair of a horse track.

"You got to understand, I been reading sign since I was old enough to walk, and I know how cattle behave. These were being driven, but there didn't seem to be a horse anywhere around. It occurred to me that someone might be going along behind them on foot, but that made no kind of sense. You go fooling around with one of those old moss-backs on foot and he'll split your gizzard quick." ¯

Mary Kay brought Nolan a cup of coffee and he took a long drink of it and let out a deep sigh before going on. "That," he said, "tastes just a little bit better than anything I've ever slid down my gullet.

"Anyway, before the day was out I'd stumbled over a dozen trails just like that . . . some with two dozen head or more, and all seemingly pushed along by a ghost. Finally I had me an idea of how it was being done an' followed one of the trails until I had me the answer.

"They were begin driven, all right, but the gents doing the driving were almighty clever. They'd wrapped something around the hooves of their horses, probably a wide, thin piece of rawhide, and if they were careful where they rode it didn't leave no kind of trail at all. If it hadn't been for all this rain I might never have figured it out."

"How'd the rain help?" Zeb asked. "I'd think it would've washed away any tracks."

"It did make a mess of things," Nolan admitted, "but it also left a lot of mud. I finally found a place where one of those fellows couldn't get around a patch of it, and his horse left a print.

"Even there the track was nothing but a round, sloppy hole in the mud, but it was enough to let me know what was going on. Darndest thing I ever saw."

"I reckon so," I said. "It's a wonder you ever made heads or tails of it. How many head do you think are missing and how old were the trails?"

Nolan shook his head. "It's bad. I reckon John could have six hundred head missing in all, but it looks like these boys only took maybe a hundred and fifty, two hundred head. At least this time around.

"As for age, some of the trails were four, five days old, but at least a couple were made some time before dawn yesterday. I came in to get a fresh horse and a few supplies, then I figure to go after them."

"I'll ride along," I said. "Seems to me they'll be holding the herd somewhere not far from John's range until they gather all they want. After that they'll head off for Mexico to turn a tidy profit."

"I don't think we have to hurry," Nolan said. "They can't push that many cattle very fast. I doubt they even expect anyone to catch on until it's too late."

"I'd like to ride along as far as Uncle John's place," Mary Kay said. "He'll be needing some personal things when he comes out of this and I can bring them back."

"Sounds all right to me," I said. "Nolan, how soon did you plan on starting back out?"

"Let me get some breakfast under my belt and swallow a

pot of coffee or two, then we can pack a bit of grub and be off."

That's the way we worked it, though Nolan was nigh as good as me at putting the food away, and by the time we had our horses saddled and ready to ride it was more than two hours from the time Nolan first walked through the door. I'd just swung into the saddle when I saw Doc Priter's rig coming down the trail. He was still a ways off, but I raised a hand in greeting and he waved in return.

We rode off toward John's place then, Nolan leading and taking a longer, more roundabout route than the one I knew.

"It's all the damn rain we've had," he said. "There's streams all over the place that a frog could've hopped a week ago, and today you'd need a boat to cross them.

"Going this way we can stick to higher ground and maybe get a look at some of the range I missed yesterday all at the same time."

Mary Kay rode along beside me, and it was all I could do to keep my eyes on the trail. She'd donned a white blouse and a pair of pants so she could straddle her horse, and she'd done something to her hair that was mighty fetching. I tell you, just looking at her made me wonder what I'd done with my summer wages.

It was maybe a shade less than twenty miles to John's spread on a straight line, but we were going farther down on North Plain and then up through the Datil Mountains from the south. The way we were going made for easier traveling, but it added several miles to our trip.

It was mighty pretty country we rode through, no doubt made more so by having Mary Kay beside me. Up in Colorado where I come from, though, the Datil Mountains wouldn't even be considered foothills. Those Rockies could've swallowed this range whole and never even burped.

We broke for a short lunch around noon and then pushed on, finally coming onto the south boundary of John's range around two in the afternoon. Here Nolan slowed the pace some and began to cut for sign as we rode. At first we found nothing, but then, not more than three miles short of John's house, we cut a trail.

Just as Nolan had described, there was no evidence of a horseman anywhere. It was as though the cattle had bunched themselves up and decided to leave home all on their own.

There were twenty head or so being pushed along, and I'd done enough tracking in my time to tell the sign was fresh. Unless I missed my guess, it had been made not more than three hours or so before we came along. Nolan looked at me and his face was hard. "I've had about enough of this," he said. "John laid up for God knows how long and these bastards bleeding him dry."

I knew how he felt. It was looking like John would live, but if things kept up at this rate he might not have a ranch to go back to. "Let's take Mary Kay on to John's place," I said, "then go read these boys from the book."

"I'll read 'em from the book," Nolan said. "I'll read 'em from the book of Colonel Colt."

We rode on to the ranch house, and the Coger boys saw us coming and met us outside. "How you boys doing?" I asked. "Not too boring around here for you, is it?"

"Not so you'd notice," Joe said. "Why, just last night we had a whole passel of fellows come by with the intent of throwing a party."

"Yeah," Jeff said. "They were in a fine mood, too. Yelling to beat the band and firing off their guns friendly like."

"What happened?" Nolan asked.

"Not much," Joe said. "We didn't want to be left out of the fun, so we naturally started firing our own guns. But you know what? Those boys didn't really want to have a good time after all. Why, we didn't get more than half a dozen shots in before they rode away like they was mad or something."

"All except one fellow," Jeff said. "He decided to stay for a spell."

"Yeah, we buried him out back," Joe added.

Mary Kay had a wide-eyed look on her face like she wasn't sure whether they were serious. Nolan had pegged those Coger brothers right, and I doubted they'd have any more riders by night for a while.

"We came across a trail a few miles back," I said. "Nolan and me intend to follow it a ways and see if we can't throw a little party of our own."

"Sounds good," Joe said. "Are we invited?"

"Sorry, Nolan and me figure to have all the dances to ourselves this time. Besides, we need one of you to stay here and the other to take Mary Kay back to her place after she gathers some of John's things."

Jeff shook his head. "Well, if that's the way it has to be, you boys have fun. I'll ride back with Miss Spencer here, if that's all right with you, Joe. I'm getting a plain case of cabin fever cooped up here all the time."

"Sure," Joe said. "Go ahead. I'll stick around here in case those boys come back."

Mary Kay looked at me. "Be careful" was all she said, but it was enough.

"We'll be fine," I said, "but there's no tellin' how long it will take. Depends on how far we have to trail them and what happens when we catch up.

"We should be back sometime late tomorrow . . . day after, at the latest."

"If you aren't," she said, "I'll come looking for you."

She would, too. Mary Kay wasn't much bigger than a minute, but there was a lot of woman tied up in that package.

It isn't often I get tongue-tied—my pa used to say I could talk a possum out of a persimmon tree—but right then I didn't know what to say. I just kind of swallowed hard, tipped my hat, and quickly rode away, Nolan right behind me.

We rode back south until we cut that trail again, and then

we followed along. They'd gained another couple of hours on us, but we rode along slow. We wanted to catch up with them, but only a fool rushes in at a time like that. Above all, we wanted to see them before they saw us.

Nolan had his Winchester out, resting it over his saddle for easy use, and I had that Colt revolving shotgun of mine near to hand. There wasn't any need to watch the trail—a blind man could've followed it—so we kept our eyes busy searching the land ahead and every possible place a man might lie in wait with a rifle.

It wasn't likely they'd know they were being followed, but anyone who'd rustle cattle in the first place would have to be suspicious by nature or he wouldn't last long.

The trail turned a little, taking us south and west onto the Plains of St. Augustine, and I was beginning to wonder what they had in mind. Mexico was near two hundred miles south, but it was wild country all the way and I knew most of the cattle rustled anywhere around would eventually reach there, but what had me puzzled was something else.

The twenty or so head we were trailing were only a tiny part of the missing cattle. We figured they must be holding the herd somewhere to the south until they had as many gathered as they could easily drive, but now I was beginning to wonder.

I put the question to Nolan and he studied it for a minute or two. "I still think they're holding the main herd somewhere," he said. "Thing is, they may be smarter than we gave them credit for.

"We figured they'd hold the cattle somewhere just off John's range until they were ready to push the whole bunch south. It's plain they aren't doing that or we'd have caught up with them by now. We've been on this trail for a good ten miles and it's still going strong.

"No, I think they decided it was too risky to hold the herd close for fear somebody might try running down one of the trails, just like we are now."

"You know this country better than I do," I said. "Where would they be holding them?"

"Well, with all this rain, water wouldn't be a problem, but they would need good grazing and someplace where the cattle wouldn't be too likely to drift.

"I'd say the other side of these plains . . . somewhere around Horse Springs, maybe. There's canyons and the like around there that would do the job proper."

"How much farther?"

"Oh, another forty miles or thereabouts. But we'd be wise to catch up with this bunch before they get there."

I didn't have to ask why. From the sign we'd found, the twenty head we were trailing were being pushed by only two men. God only knew how many would be waiting with the main herd. Two men we could handle, but I had no intention of tackling maybe a dozen or more. Not if I could help it, anyway.

"Let's push a little harder," I said. "It'll be dark before long and we can set up camp for a couple of hours, then go looking. If they don't know they're being followed they'll likely build a fire for supper. We should be able to see it for a couple of miles."

Nolan nodded and we picked up our speed a bit. When the sun dropped behind the western ridges we hunted shelter and built a tiny fire of our own. It wasn't any bigger than a man's hat, but it would do for coffee. Nolan dug into his saddlebags and came out with a handful of jerky. He tossed a couple of pieces to me.

"It won't really fill you up," he said, "but it'll keep your mouth busy and stop your stomach from worrying about it too much."

We sat there and drank a pot of coffee and chewed on jerky for a couple of hours, talking some as men around a fire will.

"That Mary Kay is quite a woman," Nolan said, "and she sure has her cap set for you."

"Me? What would a woman like that want with a poor, long-legged galoot like me? I've nothing to offer and getting less every day."

Nolan shrugged. "I reckon there are some women that would matter with," he said, "but I don't read her as one of them."

"Maybe," I said. "But it matters to me. Have you taken a look at that woman? Lord, if there's anything lovelier this side of heaven, I'll eat my hat."

"Sounds to me," Nolan said, "that you're as stuck on her as she is on you."

"Maybe," I said, "but you'll have a hard time convincing me that she'd have anything to do with a cowboy whose only home is a saddle.

"What about you?" I asked. "Why aren't you pulling double?"

Nolan poured another cup of coffee. "You know how it is out here," he said. "Women are scarce. It seems all of them are either married or spoken for."

We sat for a time without speaking, thinking our own thoughts, each wondering, I suppose, whether he would find the woman who might walk beside him. That's the thing about sitting around a campfire . . . it gives a man time to think.

And what I thought about was Mary Kay. I'd no doubt that Nolan was wrong about her being stuck on me, but what if she was? The kindest thing I could do for her would be to ride away as soon as the trouble ended. I'd been over on the lonesome side before, and Mary Kay would soon find a man who'd drive all thought of me from her head.

I dumped the rest of my coffee on the fire, then kicked dirt over the mess with my foot. "Let's go find those cattle," I said. "Time's a-wasting."

CHAPTER 12

THERE was only a sliver of moon hanging in the sky, but even that threw enough light to track twenty head of cattle. We followed along for better than two hours before we saw the soft glow of a dying fire some distance ahead.

At a quarter mile we tied our horses and went ahead on on foot. Topping a small hill, we found the cattle. They were pushed into a sort of natural corral between two hills and the rustlers had made camp at the opening.

There were only two men with the cattle and both were curled up under their blankets, fast asleep. Nolan worked the lever of his rifle gently, opening the bolt just enough to make certain a round was chambered. "Those boys are sleeping too peacefully to suit me," Nolan said. "Let's go down there and show them the error of their ways."

"Sounds good," I said.

We started to move ahead slowly when Nolan suddenly froze. "What is it?" I asked.

"Don't know. Thought I heard something."

I strained my ears at the darkness. At first I heard nothing, but then the faint, rhythmic sound of horses came to me. "Horses," I said. "More than one coming this way."

We quickly backed away and moved behind an outcropping of rock. Two more minutes passed with the sound of the horses growing steadily louder. Then two riders came into the dying firelight; they rode in from the northwest, and they came prepared to find the camp.

One of the sleeping men woke suddenly and grabbed for his gun, then stopped after he recognized the riders. He shook the other man awake while the riders dismounted and tied their horses. Someone threw an armload of wood onto the fire and it sprang to life.

We were forty yards outside the circle of light, but now we could make out faces clearly. I didn't know either of the men who had been pushing the stolen cattle, but the two riders were another story. Nolan recognized them too. "I'll be damned," he said. "Strayer and Ames."

"Now what would two of Colby Ryan's men be doing out here meeting up with cattle rustlers? Nolan, I think we have the connection we've been looking for."

"Looks like. Now all we have to do is get them back to Alamitos."

"Let's wait for first light," I said. "Give them a chance to get back to sleep. You might as well grab a few hours yourself."

"I could use it. Wake me after a spell and I'll take over the watch."

We couldn't bring our horses any nearer for fear of being heard, but Nolan walked to them and brought back our blanket rolls. He stretched his out and crawled between them. In about a minute he was sound asleep. Nolan Blocke was a man without nerves.

I settled down to watch. The men talked for fifteen minutes or so, then Ames got back in the saddle and rode off to the south. Strayer unsaddled his own horse and picketed him where he could graze, then spread his blankets out near the fire. He was a cautious man, that Strayer. When he crawled between the blankets that big Colt stayed belted around his waist.

Easing into a more comfortable position, I fought against going to sleep myself. The time passed slowly, and after three hours I shook Nolan awake. "You'd best take over," I said. "Ames rode out, but the rest are asleep."

"One less we have to deal with," Nolan said. "Likely rode to wherever the hell that main herd is to check on progress for Ryan."

Sleep didn't come quite as easily for me as it had for Nolan, but I got there. I had a fine dream about Mary Kay, but just when it was getting good Nolan shook me awake.

"It'll be light in a few minutes," he said. "We should roust those boys while they're still asleep."

I rolled my blankets and checked my shotgun, making certain the action was free and a round was chambered. Then we started down the hill toward the camp. The ground was still soft and spongy from all the rain and we made no more sound than nothing, but Strayer must have had ears like a cat. When we were still ten yards from the sleeping men he suddenly rolled and came to his feet; the Colt on his side seemed to jump from the holster. He was fast, but not nearly fast enough. Nolan tilted his rifle slightly and fired from the hip.

I plainly heard the *whump* of the bullet as it slammed into Strayer's gut. He staggered back and tried to raise his pistol for a shot, but there was no mercy in Nolan. He fired again, and if Strayer had a heart to begin with, it was no longer in condition to do the job. Strayer fell, landing face down in the hot coals of the fire. He never felt a thing.

Those other two came to their feet, but my shotgun was covering them. They were still groggy from sleep, and just like that it was all over. We tied their hands and I dragged Strayer from the fire.

Nolan dug into their supplies and commenced fixing breakfast while I went for our horses. Time I got back, bacon was sizzling in a skillet and a pone of bread was going strong in a Dutch oven.

"Checked their horses," Nolan said. "Strayer's has a pretty, star-shaped nick out of one shoe."

I grinned. Nolan had his revenge . . . and so did Evan Cory.

Those other rustlers, one short and bearded, the other long and lean, looked at us. "You just going to let us starve?" the bearded one asked.

"You'll hang before you starve," I said. "I'm not about to spoonfeed you, and I'll be damned if I'm going to cut you loose so you can feed yourself."

He didn't say anything else, just leaned back and looked off to the south. "Nolan," I said, "the way these boys keep staring off yonder way, I'm starting to wonder if they know something we don't."

"You think they're expecting company?"

"That's my thought. We'd best pack up and get out of here quick."

I saddled two horses for our captives while Nolan gathered everything else. In fifteen minutes we were ready to ride. We untied the hands of those boys and retied them in front so they could ride. We were just swinging into the saddle when Nolan pointed to the south. "Keep your eyes on that little hill about a mile straight away from my finger," he said. "I do believe that's what these boys were looking for."

I looked and it didn't take long to see a group of riders, maybe ten or twelve, come riding into view. They were coming slow and obviously hadn't noticed anything out of the ordinary yet.

"We'll have to leave the cattle," I said, "and hope we can beat that bunch back to Alamitos."

"Not likely," Nolan said. "These boys are bound to slow us down some."

"If you've any ideas," I said, "now is the time for them."

Nolan didn't hesitate. "There's some mighty rough country to the east. It's ten miles or so, but it's all standing on end and rocky as hell. If we can reach it we may be able to lose them. Assuming these two don't give us any trouble."

"They may give us trouble once," I said. "But if they do, it'll be the last time."

"Then let's get a move on. In case you hadn't noticed, that bunch is getting closer all the time."

We took off out of there like our tails were on fire, riding due east and trying to get some distance before that bunch realized that anything was wrong. After twenty minutes there was still no sign of pursuit, but that didn't mean a thing. They were back there and they were coming. I could feel it.

We got into rougher ground after a spell, and Nolan had given a pretty good description of it. I'd seen higher mountains, but I hadn't seen many that were rougher. It looked for all the world like God had tired of the process and just dropped things down and let them lie the way they fell.

Nolan took a deer trail that seemed to go right up the side of a cliff. Now, I've never been particularly afraid of heights, but in about fifteen minutes we were five hundred feet up and riding a trail so narrow that at times my outside stirrup hung over the edge. Right then I was thinking hard about turning right around and facing those boys chasing us. If I had to die, I'd rather it be from a bullet than from a long fall and a sudden stop.

Nolan kept right on climbing though, and he looked like he was going to a Sunday picnic. Those two along with us seemed to favor my point of view, however, and both had a pretty good sweat going before we topped that trail.

We came out in a high meadow, but that wasn't what Nolan was after. He skirted the edge of it, then suddenly seemed to fall out of sight just ahead. Those two rustlers were riding between us, and when they reached the point where he'd disappeared I saw their faces go white. Then they dropped from sight just as Nolan had.

When I hit the spot I reckon I blanched a bit myself. Nolan had stepped his horse off onto a long talus slope that seemed to stretch a mile down the side of that mountain. His horse hit bottom even as I watched, those other two close behind. I took a deep breath and put spurs to Cap.

Cap went off the edge, struck hard and dropped onto his tail and started sliding, his feet working like pistons to keep his balance until we slid out onto solid ground.

Nolan was already starting up another trail, and I followed. We went straight up for several hundred feet, turned off on a switchback, and at last came out on a solid piece of ground that looked like steady riding for a while.

That deer trail where we first started up was a mile or more behind us as the trail went, but I could look straight across from where we now rode and see it clearly. In a straight line it couldn't have been more than seven hundred yards or so. Just as we moved onto that level ground I saw the bunch following us start up the deer trail. They saw me at the same time and one of them upped with his rifle and let loose a shot.

Where the bullet went, I don't know, but it was nowhere near us. Shooting at that distance, and especially shooting uphill, is a tricky thing. The way that fellow's horse, and those around him, cut up when he fired gave me an idea, though, and if it worked we might gain some time.

Moving onto the level ground, I rode until well out of sight from those below, then reined in. Sliding my Winchester from the scabbard, I dropped from the saddle and handed Nolan my reins. "Ride far enough ahead to keep the horses from being riled by a few shots," I said. "I'm going to give those boys following us something to think about."

He grinned, urged on the two rustlers in front of him, and rode off. He stopped near a stand of trees three hundred yards ahead while I eased back to where I could see the deer trail. The riders—I counted eleven—were a quarter of the way up. Finding a good place, I watched and waited.

I knew that about three quarters of the way up, the trail narrowed down to nothing. I slid the rear sight of my rifle up to the highest notch and waited. When they reached the narrowest section of the trail I drew a bead and squeezed off a shot, aiming at the rider in front.

Now, I didn't figure to hit a man at that distance, and I sure didn't. But what happened was even better. My bullet struck the rock wall about two feet right in front of one of the horses. The bullet spit fragments of rock, spanging off into the air as it did.

That horse nearly went crazy. It reared up and spun around, crashing into the rider behind. That started a chain reaction and in a moment all hell broke loose on that narrow trail. One man was thrown from his horse and grabbed onto the edge for all he was worth. Behind him a horse bucked, jumped—and horse, rider, and all went over the edge.

I'll give it to those boys, though, they were horsemen. Even in the confusion they fought those horses back under control and started for the top. I leveled my Winchester and fired three more times, then got out of there without waiting for the results.

I ran to where Nolan was waiting and hopped into the saddle.

"How'd it go?" he asked.

"They're still coming," I said, "but at least one of them took the quick route down. They'll go careful from now on."

Nolan laughed and took to riding again. For the rest of that day we rode some of the roughest trails I ever want to see, and come dark we made a cold camp. Nolan handed out more of his jerky and we eased down to sleep, wore out from the days riding.

"It looks like we gave them the slip," Nolan said. "We should be able to cut for Alamitos come morning."

Our prisoners had been pretty much silent the whole ride, but now one of them spoke up. "You ain't got a chance of getting us back," he said. "By now the boss has men scattered all over the country. They don't need to track us . . . all they got to do is keep an eye on the trails leading to town."

Unfortunately, he made sense. Too much of it. "How about that, Nolan," I said. "You know, he may just be right. Might be we should just find a tree and hang 'em right here."

"Save a lot of trouble all the way around," Nolan said. "We take 'em into town and we got to go through a trial and likely ride all the way in two or three times just to give our side.

"Yes, sir. It starts looking bad and I say we just hang them from the nearest tree."

Those boys might not have believed me, but they sure enough believed Nolan. They went a little white and neither one offered another word. Truth of the matter was, we couldn't hang them, much as they deserved it. With Strayer dead and Ames still on the loose, we needed one of them to spill his guts about who their boss was.

We slept cold and hungry that night and pushed on at first light, still going east. During the afternoon we angled off north and pushed on. That evening we had a fire for the first time, and a hot meal to go with it. There was still no sign of pursuit.

By noon of the following day we were north to the point of being nearly even with Alamitos. John's ranch was only a few hours due west, and we started for it. They might be looking for us to show up there, but I was hoping they'd be looking for us to come in from the east or the south.

Just as we rode onto John's land we heard shorts, four of them, from the north. They came from a long way off, the sound carried to us on the wind, and obviously had nothing to do with Nolan or me. We pulled up and looked in that direction. "I don't like the sound of that at all," Nolan said. "It smells like trouble."

I took my hat off and ran my fingers through my hair. "Anbody live up that way?"

Nolan nodded. "That's just it. Tom Castle lives just about a mile from here. He's a tough man, quiet like, keeps to himself. He isn't the kind to go firing a gun without a reason.

"Tom has a shoestring outfit, but one of the better watering holes around is on his property. It don't count for much this time of year, but in high summer, or in a year where the rains don't come, it means a lot."

"Is that a roundabout way of saying that Ryan has an interest in his place?"

"That's about it," Nolan said. "Besides, there were at least two different guns being fired. I don't like it."

"Might be you should ride over there and see what's going on."

Nolan gestured at the two rustlers. "What about these jaspers?"

"I can handle them. It isn't far to John's place, and once there we'll be fine. Between me and the Cogers, I reckon we can handle whatever comes our way."

"If you're sure," Nolan said. "I wouldn't bother, but Tom has a niece living with him, and if there's trouble she might need help."

"I might have known there was a woman involved," I said. "Go ahead and check it out. When you've rescued your lady, meet me at John's."

Nolan grinned and got a sheepish look on his face, but he turned and rode off to the north. Me, I took a long, hard look at those rustlers. "You got any ideas," I said, "you'd best forget them. Fact is, I'm getting real tired of your company. You give me reason, any reason at all, and I'll put a bullet in your gizzards and leave you for the buzzards."

We hadn't ridden half an hour when I suddenly wished Nolan were still along. A group of riders cut the trail half a mile in front of us, traveling to the north. I turned south without hesitating.

It seemed Ryan, or whoever was leading the bunch after us, was smarter than I thought. They were putting men on all sides of John's ranch, and that meant we were cut off. The only chance was to cut south and try to sneak to Zeb's.

We rode right into the flooded country Nolan had mentioned, and although the water had gone down a bit, it was still there and was plenty deep and fast in some spots. It was rough, dangerous country at any time of year, but with all the rain it would be an easy thing for a man to drown in those fast, flooded streams.

We rode on, skirting the worst of the wet areas whenever possible, but it was no go. Again we saw riders in the hills ahead, and again I had to push south, moving away from any possible help.

Sooner or later, we were bound to run into a group of Ryan's men if we kept blundering about. What I needed was a place to hole up and sit things out. Ryan couldn't keep men in the field forever, and if I could avoid them long enough they might get the idea that I'd slipped through their line.

Off to my left, maybe a quarter mile away, a thin snake of a trail caught my eye. It seemed to go right up the side of a cliff and disappear over an outcropping that seemed stuck on the mountain like a raisin on a cake.

Taking a chance, I pointed the two rustlers that way. On closer examination, the trail proved a difficult climb for horses, but if we could get up there it might be exactly what I was looking for. Those two rustlers both turned white when I told them to start up the trail, but the tone in my voice left no room for argument, and they started up.

It wasn't long before I was questioning my decision. The trail was probably made by deer, and it was a tight go for a horse. Several times rocks rattled out of place, dislodged by the hooves of the horses, and once the bearded rustler near went over the edge when one of the falling rocks spooked his gelding.

Then we were up the trail and over the outcropping. The trail dipped into a hollow that covered nearly half an acre. There was a pool of water and some rough mountain grass that would feed the horses for a while, and I doubted any of Ryan's men would even consider us being up there, let alone risk that trail to find out.

CHAPTER 13

I'D no intention of staying in that hollow any great length of time, but the time I was there needed to be put to good use. First thing I did was strip the saddles from the horses and picket them where they might eat a little grass and drink from the pool of rainwater.

That mountain grass wouldn't last long, but the rest alone would do the horses good, and a fresh horse can make all the difference.

A hot meal and a hot cup of coffee were in the front of my mind, but I was afraid to risk a fire. Up high like we were, with no trees or the like to scatter the smoke, a fire could be seen for miles. The way those two rustlers grumbled, a hot meal was pretty high up on their list of priorities, too, but we all settled for jerky and rainwater.

Times like that a man's stomach seems to do his thinking for him, and my thoughts turned back to the last good meal I'd eaten . . . or rather to the woman who cooked it.

I'd been thinking about Mary Kay since the moment I met her, and now, alone in those wild hills with only myself to depend on, surrounded by men intent on killing me, it seemed that Mary Kay filled my mind more and more. It was a dangerous thing. When I should have been thinking about how to get out of those hills alive, planning what I would do next, trying to anticipate what Ryan's men would do next, I was thinking about Mary Kay.

And I was thinking about her in terms that I'd been afraid to use before. I'd never been in love . . . not even in the silly way that most boys fall in love when they reach that age where girls are suddenly more exciting than hunting bear.

But love was the word that kept springing to mind whenever I thought of Mary Kay. That it was a foolish thought, I knew. That as friendly as she might be to me, a woman like that would have nothing to do with me in a marrying way, I knew. But there it was in my mind, and I couldn't seem to let it go.

Taking my spyglass, I moved up to the edge of the hollow and commenced looking the country over, working a piece of iron-hard jerky over with my teeth as I looked. Up high as I was, it was possible to see for miles even without the spyglass. Slowly, carefully, I examined the countryside.

For a long time I saw nothing, and then, with darkness only an hour away, a wispy movement caught my eye. After a few moments I realized I was looking at a tendril of smoke rising from a campfire. It was a mile or more away, and it blended in against the gray rock of the background, but through the spyglass it was clear enough to be certain.

I knew that this was only one of several groups Ryan would have after us by now, but if I could put them out of action it would at least cut the odds a bit. It would take some thought. Biting off another chunk of jerky, I settled back to give it some.

There would almost certainly be too many for me to fight, but fighting wasn't what I had in mind. If I could drive off their horses, maybe dust them some, make them spend the next day chasing horses instead of me, I'd count myself lucky.

Any gunfire would also draw other of Ryan's men to the area, but that could be to my advantage. If another bunch of riders or two came charging in to see what the shooting was about, it might let me ride around and slip through their line all the easier.

I fought with myself for a spell, weighing both sides and trying to decide whether the risk was worth it. At last I decided it was. Retying the rustlers, hands and feet, I gagged them with their own bandannas, then started out of the hollow and down the trail with the last light of the day.

It was easier going down the trail on foot than it had been going up it on horseback, but it still wasn't pleasant. Time I reached the bottom I was ready to swear off mountains forever.

It was wet, broken, rugged country that I traveled over to reach that campfire, and it took time. An hour passed, then another, but at last I was lying on a high-up ridge looking down at a camp of Ryan's men. I counted eight men around the fire, then spotted two posted as guards.

The first guard was atop a boulder maybe fifty yards to the north of the camp. He was visible only as an outline in the darkness. Even as I watched he went from a standing to a sitting position, making himself comfortable against the long watch.

The other guard was twenty-five yards south of the camp, there to guard the horses tied on a picket line. He was leaning against a tree, watching the camp, and had little mind for his duties. Good. That should make it easier.

I wasn't about to hit the camp while they were awake and alert, so I settled back and waited. The fire slowly burned lower, and one by one the men rolled into their blankets and went to sleep. An hour passed and the fire was only a red bed of coals.

It was time to make my move. The guard sitting on that boulder was my first target, so I stalked through the darkness, taking my time and making no sound. I came up behind him, moving an inch at a time, placing each foot carefully before putting my weight on it.

At the last second the guard must have sensed me. He started to turn, but it was too late. I grabbed the back of his collar and jerked. He came off the boulder and hit the ground hard enough to knock the wind from his lungs.

He wheezed and tried to struggle, but I didn't have time to mess with him. I laid the barrel of my Colt alongside his jaw and he went limp. Taking a moment to tie him with a piggin' string, I started for the other guard.

Cover was more abundant on his side of the camp, and he was easier to approach, but he was also much closer to the camp and I couldn't risk the noise of a struggle. Moving up behind the guard, I placed the cold muzzle of my rifle very gently against the bare skin behind his ear.

He drew a sharp breath, but made no other sound. "How much do you want to live?" I asked softly.

"Just tell me what to do."

"Prop your rifle against the tree and walk ahead of me."

He did just that, giving me no trouble at all. When I had him out of sight from the camp, I tied him as I had the other guard.

Moving to the horses, I took my knife from the sheath and cut through the picket line. That knife was made for me by a man who knew his business and was razor sharp. I keep it in a sheath down the back of my neck where I can reach it easily and throw it, all in one move.

Gathering the reins in my hands, I led the horses into the night, keeping one eye on the camp in case someone awoke. They didn't. I walked the horses two hundred yards, then cut the reins and sent them running with a sharp smack of my hand. They mightn't go far, but with no reins Ryan's men would have to ride them with hackamores if they did find them.

That done, I set about looking for more mischief to make. It was crazy and well I knew it, but I eased back to the camp and moved among the sleeping men. By the time I left I'd managed to quietly gather half a dozen rifles and three Colts. I dumped them off a cliff and made my way back to where I left the rustlers.

I grabbed a few hours sleep, awoke before dawn, and saddled the horses. We came out of the hollow and started down the trail before it was full daylight.

Trouble was, I just didn't know the trails or the country

well enough. I knew the direction I wanted to go, northwest toward Zeb's, but I had to take the trails as I found them and hope they didn't dead-end . . . or lead me into an ambush.

It was far from easy going, and several times I had to backtrack and find a new trail when the one we were on turned off in the wrong direction. Those two rustlers undoubtedly knew which trails to take, but it was in their best interest to keep me from reaching Alamitos and I couldn't trust them.

Even with the false trails we made progress. Every so often I'd find a spot of high ground where I might look the country over through my spyglass, but each time I saw nothing. I knew Ryan's men were still out there, but not once did I see any sign of them. That made me nervous. From all I'd seen there must have been at least four or five groups of men searching for us, but I saw nothing.

The smart thing would have been to hole up and wait them out. Sooner or later they'd figure we'd slipped through, or Nolan would put together some men of his own and come out to get us. But like I said, I never laid claim to being smart. Stubborn and ornery as any mule, yes, but never smart.

And it was a good thing I never made such a claim, cause right then I did something stupid. I took a trail that I shouldn't have taken, and I took it without taking the time to scout it first. Might be I wouldn't have seen anything if I had found a high spot and looked it over, but the thing is I didn't do it. And we rode right into the hot side of hell.

We were right in the heart of the wettest part of that country, and the trail I took was maybe halfway between Zeb and John's ranches. That's where they found us.

The trail was just a wide spot alongside a mountain that cattle and deer had worn into a passable road. To our right the mountain swept upward several hundred feet, and to our left it turned abruptly into a sheer drop of three hundred feet.

It wasn't really a cliff. A fast-moving stream at the bottom of the mountain, swollen and filled with mud and debris, had cut the earth away over the years to form a slick cut from the mountainside. A few more years and the very trail we rode on would be washed away.

The mountainside above us was covered by thick stands of pine, with boulders from an old rockslide scattered here and there among them. It was perfect for an ambush.

We were halfway across the mountainside when at least six men suddenly popped from behind the boulders, and every mother's son held a gun. I acted without thought, drawing my Colt and firing at the nearest man the moment he appeared. Even as I fired I slapped Cap with my spurs.

But there was no cover and we had too far to go. Flame spouted from behind the boulders and something struck me hard in the side. Only an instant later the sun seemed to explode inside my head. Then I was falling.

Falling right over the edge of that muddy cliff with three hundred feet of nothing below me, I hit hard, slid a long way, bounced outward, then hit again. One last time I struck, bounced, then the cold water of the stream sucked me in.

I went all the way to the bottom, tried to fight to the surface, but something grabbed at my feet. I jerked free an instant before my lungs could take no more. At last I broke the surface and gulped for air.

I managed to draw in a shallow breath before I was sucked under again, but it was enough to hold me until I once more broke the surface. The water was trying to pull me under, but I struck out and grabbed a handful of water, trying to swim to the bank. I saw the boulders, jagged edges breaking the surface of the muddy water, too late, and slammed into them hard. Something struck me a wicked blow alongside the head and blackness closed in.

The last thing I remembered was the face behind one of the rifles. It belonged to Dan Ames.

Should have killed him before he rode away from that

rustler's camp, I thought, should have killed him sure. Now I'll never have the chance.

Somewhere between life and death, I could still feel the rush of the water as it carried me down to wherever it was going, and I could still feel the cold. *This must be what it's like to die* popped into my head. Then there was nothing. No water, no cold, no thoughts . . . just a bottomless pit of blackness.

CHAPTER 14

WHEN I opened my eyes I was lying face down on a gravel bank at the edge of the stream. Most of my legs were still in the water and I was cold. Colder than I'd ever been. Colder than I would have believed possible.

My head throbbed and a red light seemed to flash in front of my eyes with each pulse of my head. My side hurt like hell and my left hand, resting on the gravel in front of my face, was a bruised bloody mass.

I tried to move and nothing happened. That scared me and I tried harder. This time my right arm moved, but it was like a dead thing with no feeling at all. I found I could roll my body a little from side to side, so that's what I did, over and over and over again.

The feeling slowly came back to my arms, but it was far from a pleasant experience. It was like a million red hot needles jabbing each arm, in fact, but eventually the pain eased, and my arms and hands began to respond to my will. My legs were still dead and useless, but I had to move.

Slowly extending my hand, I grabbed a handful of ground and pulled. It was an inch at a time with long rests between pulls, but after a spell I had both legs out of the water. Alternately pulling and rolling back and forth to wake up my legs, I reached dry ground. At that point I just turned loose and passed out again.

When I opened my eyes for the second time I was still weak as a kitten, but the sun had partially dried my clothing and I no longer felt like a chunk of ice. My legs weren't exactly up to dancing, but they would at least move.

I felt better, but I was still scared. I had no idea of how

bad I was really hurt, but it seemed certain that at least two bullets had struck me, one in the right side and the other in the head. I'd undoubtedly lost more blood than I could spare, but it was the water and the cold that really scared me.

If a fever set in it would almost certainly kill me unless I found shelter and warmth. I still was a ways from being able to walk, but I could crawl and did so. My target was a shadow among the rocks some fifty yards ahead that might have been a hollow or even a cave.

It took the better part of an hour, but at last I reached the rocks. What I'd been looking at was a hollow, nothing more than a twelve-foot-deep hole in the side of a cliff, but it would keep out the wind and I'd be dry if it should rain again.

I crawled inside and dropped to my stomach, breathing like I'd run a mile, and tried to catch my wind. After a few minutes I rolled onto my back and began going through my pockets in an effort to check my resources. My gunbelt had been ripped away in the fall and I'd lost both boots, but somehow my cigar case remained in my pocket. Now if only the matches inside were still dry enough to light.

They were. I crawled about gathering dry leaves and sticks until I had a respectable pile, then struck a match and coaxed a fire into life. The heat reflected off the rock around me and in no time at all I was warm. Thing was, it would be dark in two or three hours, and in my shape I'd have trouble keeping the fire going.

I'd nothing to boil water in, but I set about checking my wounds as best I could. I had a bullet hole in my right side, where the bullet had gone in and exited only a couple of inches farther back. It wasn't serious unless infection set in, but it was still bleeding a little, no doubt from the strain of crawling around.

With my fingers I examined the back of my head and felt a deep groove where a bullet had grazed my skull. The bleeding had stopped from that one, but my head still hurt like hell and that red light was still blinking in time with my pulse.

I could barely use my left arm, and when I'd squirmed free of my shirt it was easy to see why. My shoulder and arm were a solid black and blue from top to bottom. That likely came from bouncing down that cliff and smashing into rocks while being washed down that stream.

It hurt like anything to move, but it didn't feel like anything was broken.

I'd been far luckier than I had any right to be, hurt though I was. But without food and proper care that wouldn't matter. Somehow I had to get help and soon. It was too late to do much about it before dark, but come morning I'd have to light out for Zeb's.

A terrible thirst was starting to parch my throat, from the loss of blood most likely, and I knew I was going to have to work my way back down to that stream before anything else. I'd had enough of crawling for one day, so I hunted till I found a stick of the proper length and used it for a crutch, failing several times, but at last making it to my feet.

It wasn't pretty, but I hobbled down to that stream and got me a good long drink. While my face was buried in the water a glint caught my eye and I reached for it, coming up with my sheath knife. It must have fallen free as I struggled to crawl from the stream.

Slipping it back in place, I drank some more, then hobbled back to my fire. That fire worried me some in itself. I sure enough needed it, but it was throwing a lot of smoke . . . smoke that might be spotted by the wrong eyes.

Ryan's men probably thought me dead—by rights I should have been—but seeing the smoke from a fire they would certainly come looking for its source. And when they found it, and me, they'd finish the job right.

Without knowing the country better than I did, there was no way to tell exactly how far I was from Zeb's, but I doubted it was more than ten or twelve miles. Normally, that would be little more than a good stretch of the legs, but in my condition it may as well have been Canada.

The fire was getting low and I added more wood to it, willing to risk being seen in exchange for the warmth. Leaning against the rock wall, I got as comfortable as possible and lit a damp cigar. After a time I stubbed it out and tried to think of a course of action.

Somewhere in the middle of my thoughts I fell asleep. The dream I had was of Mary Kay. We were sitting together under a shady tree. Her head was resting on my shoulder and we were holding hands. She looked up at me and I kissed her softly on the lips. They tasted like wild honey.

The dream broke and I woke up. I was cold again, but my head was hot beneath my hand and the thirst was stronger than ever. Sure as anything I had a fever, and that was next door to dying. I tried to get up on that crutch again, but I was too weak, so I took to crawling.

I reached the stream and drank long and deep, but down inside I knew I wasn't going to make it back to the fire. My strength was gone, used up, and so was I. "Mary Kay," I said aloud, "I wish we could have . . ."

I heard the sound of a harsh laugh and then a man's voice coming from somewhere behind me. With an effort I turned over. Leon Pratt was standing not twenty yards away. He walked closer and dropped to one knee beside me.

"The boys rode into town this afternoon and told the boss they'd killed you," he said, "but Mr. Ryan wanted to make sure. He sent me out to find the body.

"You know, the boys weren't far wrong at that. Judging by the way you look, you're a lot closer to dying than to living."

He pulled a long, slim-bladed knife from a sheath and felt the sharpness of the blade with his thumb. "So you're the big, dangerous gunfighter that Mr. Ryan was so afraid of. Well, you don't look so dangerous now." He moved the knife close to my stomach. "I've always wondered how loud a man could scream. How about it, you got enough life left in you to scream?"

I was too weak and sick to stop him, but I figured to let him know how I felt about it. I summoned all the saliva in my mouth and spit right in his face. It caught him in the eye and he near fell, caught his balance, and raised the knife, his face now a hideous mask.

He started to bring the knife down into my stomach and I was certain I'd used the last of my chips. A rifle thundered somewhere close by and the knife froze. Leon's eyes opened wide and his mouth formed a question. Then he collapsed like a rag doll.

The crunch of a booted foot on gravel made me turn my head. The figure standing there was a pulsing red blur. I squinted and things cleared a little. To my fevered eyes it looked for all the world like Mary Kay. "I was just dreaming about you," I said.

Cool hands touched my face and everything faded. For a long time I knew nothing else.

CHAPTER 15

FOR long days I remember nothing but flashes of light, images of first one face and then another in front of me. Always, though, Mary Kay would be there when my eyes opened. Her hands were cool, soft, and comforting.

And then one morning I opened my eyes and they stayed open. My head was clear, and though I was weak, almighty weak, it seemed I would live. It took a minute to place where I was, but I'd enough sense to do it after a while. It was a back room of Zeb's place, one that Mary Kay used for a bedroom.

I was lying in a bed, a comfortable one, and I had to ponder a spell before I decided to move. I tell you, I could've stayed right there and done nothing for a long time. But it wasn't in me to lie a-bed more than was needed.

The first thing I tried to do was sit up. Every muscle in my body screamed at the effort and I let out a loud grunt. Instantly the door opened and Mary Kay ran in, a worried look on her face. I was still trying to sit up and she near jumped on me, pushing me back to the bed. "I might have known it," she said. "Try to save a man's life and the moment he wakes up he tries to undo it all."

I was still weak enough for her to handle, and besides, it felt real good lying there in bed being pampered by her. "Sorry," I said. "I'll stay right here and be a good boy."

"You will if you know what's good for you. Doc Priter said you'd have died out there in the mountains if you weren't so muleheaded."

"That's always been a fault of mine. I guess I did come

close to losing it out there. You know, I actually thought you were standing over me with a rifle."

Mary Kay looked down and didn't say anything. Zeb picked that moment for coming through the door and had heard what I said. "You weren't seeing things," he said. "She was out there all right, and it's a good thing she had that rifle. She put a bullet right through that Pratt fellow's gizzard before he could carve you up.

"That ain't all, either. Somehow or another, she got you on a horse and made it back here with you. Near twelve miles over the roughest country you ever saw, and all in the dark."

Me, I was flabbergasted. You got to understand, Mary Kay wasn't but an inch over five feet and maybe a hundred and twenty-five pounds. I'm six two and weigh better than two hundred pounds.

"How in the world did you ever get me on a horse," I said. "And come to think of it, what in blue hell were you doing out in that country by yourself in the first place?"

Mary Kay looked at me out of those big, green eyes, and she was dead serious when she spoke. "I warned you," she said, "that I'd come looking if you were late. When you didn't show up on time I decided to ride over to John's place, thinking maybe you were there.

"I was about halfway there when I heard a whole volley of shots off to the south. I knew there was only one trail over that way, and maybe it was foolish, but I decided to go see what it was all about.

"I found your horse running loose and backtracked him until I came to the place where you went over the edge. I found a way down and started following the stream. I'm not much good at that kind of thing, but I saw the smoke from your fire and that led me to you.

"As for getting you on your horse, you helped quite a bit, and once there, you stuck like glue."

I slowly shook my head. That woman was amazing, and no two ways about it. "What about Leon Pratt?"

"I . . . I didn't know who he was," she said. "When I first saw you he was standing some distance away. Then he walked closer and I pulled my rifle out.

"I've never shot a rifle enough to be any good . . . maybe half a dozen times all told. I was afraid if I tried to shoot him I'd hit you instead. Then he pulled out that knife. I just pointed and shot, hoping to scare him away. Somehow the bullet hit him."

"You saved my life," I said, with disbelief and gratitude.

Mary Kay took my hand and held it. Her own hand was the tiniest thing you ever saw. Small, delicate, soft, yet obviously strong enough to do what had to be done.

The bedroom door opened again and John Lysander walked in. He was still a little drawn, and thin as a rail, but he looked a whole sight better than he had the last time I saw him. He sat down in a chair near the bed and grinned.

"Some folks just can't stay out of trouble," he said. "How you feeling, son?"

I glanced at Mary Kay. "Not too bad, all things considered."

"I reckon I can understand that," he said. "Was I a young buck like you, I might give you a run for your money with that girl."

I laughed. "You stick to your own territory," I said. "The shape I'm in now, you might pull it off anyway."

"Not a chance," Mary Kay said. "I didn't drag you all the way back here just to let you get away without a fight."

I swallowed hard and looked back at John. "I'm sorry about turning up late."

He stoked up a corncob pipe. "Ask me," he said, "you timed it just about right. Those bastards up on the hill would have had me sure if you hadn't showed when you did. For that matter, I'd have bled to death in another couple of hours."

"It seems to me you're up and about awful quick," I said. "Just a couple of days back you were near death's door."

"Huh," John said. "How long do you think you've been in that bed, anyway?"

"I don't know. I guess a day or two."

"Closer to two weeks," Zeb said. "And you were gone three days or so before that. Your own wounds are near healed, though I'll bet it hurts some to move."

"*Two weeks!* I've been in this bed for two weeks?"

"Yep," John said. "And Mary Kay never leaving your side for more than a few minutes at a time. I'll tell you, having a woman like that keeping you shaved and bathed, holding your hand and forcing hot soup down you to keep you alive, I don't know, sounds like it might be worth a couple of bullet holes and a little fever."

One word in John's speech jumped out at me. That word was "bathed." I was under the blankets and wearing a kind of nightshirt, but other than that I was buck naked. "You *bathed* me!"

Mary Kay didn't blush a lick. "I wasn't going to sit in here for ten days with you growing riper by the hour. Besides, you opened your eyes once or twice while I was at it, and you didn't seem to mind then."

There's a time to argue, and there's a time to just shut up and take your medicine. And come to think of it, with the kind of medicine Mary Kay had, taking it was a pleasure.

But two weeks? I'd lost two weeks at a time when the whole county threatened to blow up anytime at all. I told them about the ambush out on the trail and asked what all had happened since I'd been out of action.

"While you three are catching up on the news," Mary Kay said, "I'm going to fix some breakfast." She looked at me. "I guess you're probably hungry by now?"

You know, I hadn't been until she mentioned it, but once the thought came to mind my stomach let me know that food was an immediate necessity. "I think I could eat a little," I said. "You know how I am . . . never much of an appetite."

Mary Kay rolled her eyes and Zeb groaned. "You've got a

small appetite, all right," Zeb said. "When those cattle buyers in Alamitos find out you're going to live, beef prices will double."

Mary Kay went out to start breakfast and Zeb started filling in the blank spots. There were a lot of them. "Don't really know where to start," he said. "But to begin with, we kind of kept it quiet about you still being alive. Outside of us and Doc Priter, only Nolan, Van Dorn, and the mayor know about it. Ryan is likely celebratin' your death still.

"Nolan took the job of county sheriff when nobody else stepped up to claim it, but he made it plain to Van Dorn that once you were able, he'd turn the badge over to you.

"The rest of the news is all bad. When Nolan left you out there to ride over to the Castle spread, he found Tom Castle dead and his niece, Julie, wounded. Con Ferris killed Tom, wounded Julie more or less accidental, then left her for dead. Nolan swears he'll see Ferris dead or in jail, but since that happened he's disappeared.

"He's still about, though, cause Simon Kearns turned up with two bullets in his chest. Young Eddie has taken over the ranch and he's fit to be tied. Bill Flynn has kept him under control, but soon or late, he'll try to tackle Ryan."

John emptied his pipe. "You know Harry Morgan, don't you?" I nodded. "Well," John said, "somebody tried to burn his saloon down a few days back. Threw a bucket of kerosene on the back wall and struck a match to it.

"Luckily for Harry, some fellow was taking a shortcut through the alley behind his place at just the right time. They got 'er put out quick, but Harry's some kind of mad. He figures Ryan is the only man in town with reason to try burning his saloon."

"Seems to me Ryan is making more enemies than he can handle."

"Might be," Zeb said, "but he don't seem none too worried about it. He's wheelin' and dealin' more than ever. And the way he's courting those rich cattle folk, you can bet he has something planned for them. Was I them, I'd keep my eyes open and my hand on my wallet."

We talked until Mary Kay had breakfast ready. Then she carried in a tray piled high with food and chased John and Zeb out. She sat down next to me and started feeding me. I tried fighting her off at first, thinking that was one chore I could do for myself, but she was one woman you just didn't fight. Figuring the only way I was going to get on the outside of any food, I finally leaned back and let her do it.

A big cup of black coffee went along with the food, and when I got a long drink of that I felt like I might live after all. I'll tell you, if anything in the world tasted half as good as Mary Kay looked, it was that first drink of hot coffee.

By the time I had my fill of food and coffee, Mary Kay was getting arm weary from shoveling it down, and probably sorry she'd started the whole thing to begin with. When I was full at last, I kind of eased out on the bed and stretched, feeling half-grateful for being shot. "If you could cook like that on a regular basis," I said, "I'd ask you to marry me."

"I can," she said. "And I'll hold you to that promise."

Someday I might learn to watch what I said around her, but it didn't look like it would be soon.

I stayed in bed the rest of the day, slowly stretching a bit of the stiffness from my body, but by evening I'd had all I could stand. It was like tackling a mad grizzly to get my clothes from Mary Kay, but when she saw that I was as determined as she was, she gave in. "Go ahead and get dressed," she said, "but if you get sick again you can take care of yourself. I won't lift a finger to help you."

"Sure you will," I said. "You enjoy it."

She grunted and walked out of the room. I doubted it would happen often, but I'd finally gotten in the last word.

It took some doing, but I got dressed and pulled on my boots, then half walked, half hobbled out to the front porch. My body told me quick that I'd gone far enough, and I dropped into Zeb's rocking chair.

Zeb and John came out and sat with me, and Mary Kay even got over her mad long enough to bring me a cup of coffee. "Supper will be ready in half an hour," she said. "If you're well enough to get out of bed, you're well enough to eat at the table."

"You know, now that you mention it," I said, "I am feeling a mite peaked. Might be I should go back to bed and let you feed me."

"You can go back to bed and lay there until you starve to death, for all I care," she said. "You'll feed yourself or you won't eat."

I closed my eyes and moaned, then slipped down in the chair a little. Mary Kay jumped down beside me and grabbed my hand.

"What's wrong," she asked. "Are you all right?"

I opened my eyes and smiled at her. "Just wanted to see if you really do care," I said.

Zeb had once told me that Mary Kay had Irish in her blood, and now it came out full force. Her mouth set and her green eyes flashed like a lightning bolt on a dark night. Then she hauled off and hit me right on my sore shoulder. I yelped for real and she stomped back to the kitchen, muttering something very unkind about men in general and me in specific.

I ate supper at the table, though, and Mary Kay never said a word the whole while. She didn't look mad, but I could almost see the wheels turning behind those pretty eyes, and unless I missed my guess, it was pure revenge turning them.

By the time I had my fill of supper I was more than ready for more of that bed. Stripping down to the buff again, I slipped between the covers and was asleep as soon as my head hit the pillow.

It was that damn rooster that woke me up again, and I made up my mind to settle things with him before much more time passed. Coming to a sitting position, I realized I felt a good deal stronger than I had last night. All that food had done me good, and it seemed a shame to stay in bed.

I dressed quietly and went outside. A quick shave in the wash basin and a few deep breaths of the cool morning air perked me right up. My left arm was still a sickly yellow from the fading bruises, my right side was stiff, and I had to be real careful in settling my hat down over that groove in my scalp, but for the most part I felt ready to tackle anything.

Nolan Blocke rode in just a little past noon, a silver star pinned to his shirt. "Wondered where you were keeping yourself," I said. "That badge must be keeping you busy."

"It does that," he said. "I can't tell you how happy I'll be when you take it over."

"When I do," I said, "you're going to be my deputy."

"Serves me right," he said. He turned serious. "Look, I'm sure sorry I rode off out there on the trail. If we'd stayed together you might not have been shot."

"If we'd stayed together," I said, "both of us might have been killed. Besides, from what I hear you were right to check out that shooting. Forget it."

"Thing I wanted to talk to you about," Nolan said, "is this. Dan Ames showed his face in town yesterday, so Ryan must have decided you're dead after all, in spite of what happened to Pratt.

"I thought hard about hauling Ames in for rustling and for taking a shot at you, but then decided against it. In the first place, if I charged him with trying to kill you they'd get the idea quick that you're still alive."

"Sounds like you have another reason," I said. "What is it?"

"Well, if you're going to be able to pin on this badge before long, I thought you might like the pleasure of throwing him in jail yourself."

"You thought right. And Ames is important. The only way we can pin any of this on Ryan is to have somebody talk, and right now Ames is our best bet. Now I've got a question for you. Since you're wearing that badge, Burack must be out of a job. How'd he take being fired?"

"Not like you'd expect. He just took his badge off, tossed it on the desk, and walked out. Never seemed upset in the least."

That did surprise me. It wasn't like Burack to take something like that lying down. He was a man I'd keep my eye on.

We sat around the table for a couple of hours talking with Zeb, John, and Mary Kay, but then Nolan stood up and reached for his hat. "I got to be getting back to town," he said.

"You're more than welcome to stay and have supper here," Mary Kay said. "You can spend the night if you'd like."

"Thanks, but Julie, ah, Miss Castle, asked me if I'd have supper with her tonight."

"Sounds like you have the inside track," I said. "Is she pretty?"

"Now what kind of question is that?" Mary Kay said. "What matters is the kind of person she is, not whether she looks good to you or Nolan."

"That's true, ma'am," Nolan said. "And she is a fine lady and a wonderful person." He looked at me and winked. "Pretty, too. Built for speed, and you never saw such blonde hair."

Mary Kay's mouth dropped open. "You men are all alike," she said. "You think more of the wrapping than the present inside."

A couple of smart replies came to mind, but I didn't want to press my luck. "It isn't that," I said. "I was just hoping he'd found somebody like you . . . beautiful inside and wrapped nice to boot."

"That," she said, "is the nicest thing you have ever said to me."

"There's a lot more I'd like to say, but I'm not much good at it. Reckon I've spent too much of my time out on the range. I never was much hand at talking to a lady."

"You do fine," she said. "When you settle down and say what you really feel, you do just fine."

Nolan planted his hat on his head and went on back to town, and as much as I liked spending time with Mary Kay, I wished I was riding along with him. Having that badge pinned to his shirt made Nolan a target, and too many men wanted to see if they could be the first to score a bull's-eye.

Right there I decided I'd lazed around long enough. Another day or two to let myself mend and I was riding into Alamitos.

CHAPTER 16

I LET another day go past just sitting and healing, then decided to get down to business. My wounds were coming along fine, but I was still stiff and sore. The trouble with that came in trying to handle my Colt.

It wasn't good enough to just be able to draw and fire it, I had to be able to draw, fire, and hit in one smooth motion, and my stiffness was slowing me down. Not a lot, but enough to get me killed. I had to work the stiffness out, and there wasn't much time to do it.

Come the morning of the second day after Nolan rode out, I scrapped up every tin can on the place, dug out all the .45 cartridges I could find, and got serious. Finding a hillside a hundred yards from the house that made for a safe backdrop, I set up those tin cans, moved twenty yards away, and adjusted that Colt so it felt right on my hip.

Now there's all manner of ways to wear a Colt, and all of them are good for a fast draw, depending on the man doing it. Some men wore a gun on the opposite side for a cross-draw, a few reversed the gun, wearing it backward and twisting their hands around to draw. Some tilted the holster forward and snapped their wrists; others wore the holster low and others high. Several times I'd met men who wore shoulder holsters and did a fine job getting it out fast and smooth when needed.

A few seldom wore a holster at all, preferring to tuck their pistol behind their belt or a sash tied around their waist.

The way I did it was common enough, as good as any other way and better than most. I favored a .45-caliber Colt 1873 Peacemaker with a four-inch barrel. I wore it straight

135

up and down with the grip about four inches above my hanging wrist. That lets the hand gather momentum as it moves up to grasp the pistol for a quick draw.

Now, standing there facing that hillside, I made certain the holster was firmly in place and tied to my leg, then I started drawing. I wasn't after speed at first, just pulling the Colt out slow and easy, not firing, but working some of the stiffness from my side and arm.

As the stiffness left, I increased my speed. The thumb slams into the hammer, cocking it before the Colt moves, fingers curl around the grip and lift the heavy pistol, trigger finger extended until it clears leather and comes level. At that point you touch the trigger for the first time, right at hip level, and if you're any good, you can shoot once at that point.

Then you bring the Colt up to eye level and look across the sights at your target, both eyes open, and fire again.

After half an hour of this I was ready to start firing live ammunition. Normally, for safety, I'd only carry five rounds in the Colt, but now I added a sixth bullet. I put my Colt in the holster and picked my first target, an empty tomato can with a red and white label.

At that moment I realized for the first time that I had an audience. I'd been concentrating so hard on what I was doing that I hadn't seen Zeb, John, and Mary Kay walk out to check up on me. That was bad enough, but Nolan was also there, grinning like a bear in a blueberry patch.

"Looks like I got here just in time," he said. "I always wanted to see how a real *pistolero* handles a gun."

"No you don't," I said. "You aren't getting off that easy. I've heard you're pretty fast yourself. Get over here beside me . . . about ten feet to my left."

Nolan moved up to the spot I indicated, spread his legs, and slipped the thong from his Colt. "The tomato can is mine," I said. "You take the peaches. John, you call it."

For twenty seconds there was absolute silence, then John suddenly yelled, *"Draw."*

Me, I just drew and fired three times, the shots very close together. My first bullet jumped the can ten feet in the air and the next two sailed in completely over the hill. Nolan stood there, his Colt half out of the holster, and he whistled. He lowered the Colt back in place and looked at me. "We are friends, aren't we?"

"Sure," I said. "What made you ask that?"

"Just want to be certain," he said. "You are one man I do not want mad at me. I never thought it was possible for anyone to be that fast."

"You've plenty of speed yourself," I said. "You just need to work on techique."

We spent the next two hours drawing and firing. Time to time I helped Nolan adjust his holster or changed his grip a bit, and before long he was close, very close, to being as fast as I was.

We burned powder until the only cartridges we had left were the ones in our gunbelts. We quit then, both of us pouring sweat, and I knew I was ready for what lay ahead as I was ever going to be.

We walked back to the house and I dropped in a chair to get some rest, and we began talking about how we were going to go about switching the badge from Nolan to me, then go about cleaning up Alamitos.

"That's one of the reasons I rode out here," Nolan said. "Ames is in town, got himself a room at the Bon Ton, but word has it that he may be skipping out soon. Could be Ryan is getting nervous."

"Then we'd better get the ball rolling."

"If Ames gets away it could slow us down to the point where Ryan might be untouchable. We get Ames in jail and make him talk, we can haul Ryan in and finish it."

"It might not be that easy. Ryan's lost some men, but he

still has enough hired guns to make everything real sticky if he cuts them loose."

"I've been thinking about that," I said, "and I may have the answer. How many men can you get together quietly by dawn? They don't have to be gunmen, but they do have to be steady and closemouthed."

"Hard to say exactly. Eight or ten for sure, maybe a few more. Why?"

I explained my plan to him quickly, going into detail only where it mattered. When I finished, Nolan let out a sigh. "It just might work at that," he said, "but I can see I'm not going to get much sleep tonight. The tough part is going to be getting all the town council in on it without somebody spilling the beans."

"Talk to them one at a time," I said. "And only the council. Chet Watkins isn't to know, and for that matter neither should Doc Priter. I trust him, and you can make him one of the men we need to enforce things, but only the council is to know about the rest of it."

"I'll do my best," he said. "Are you sure you can slip into town without being seen? That could spoil the whole deal."

"I'll time it so I get in a little before dawn," I said. "Even the dogs ought to be asleep then."

"We'll be ready for you," Nolan said. "It'll take some doing, but between Van Dorn and me, I think we can get it done."

Nolan rode out and I walked down to the barn to check on Cap. He was in a stall near the back and I gave him a good rubdown, running the curry comb through his hair from top to bottom. Topping it off with a bucket of grain, I patted him on the neck and left the stall.

When I turned to leave the barn, Mary Kay was standing there, a serious look on her face.

"It's going to start all over again, isn't it," she said. "The shooting and killing, I mean."

"It never really stopped," I said. "I just wasn't in the game for a while."

"I guess that's what I really meant. Even with you hurt, these past couple of weeks have been good. At least you were safe. Now you're going right back into it. The next time somebody shoots at you they'll probably kill you."

"It could happen," I said. "But I take a lot of killing."

"James," she said, "there's something I need to know. How do you feel about me? The truth."

I took a deep breath and let it out slow. "I'm not much good with fancy words," I said. "All I know is that when I look at you it's like every dream I ever had is standing right in front of me.

"I'm nothing but a big, homely country boy with nothing to make a woman like you happy. I own a horse, a saddle, a couple of guns, and the clothes on my back. That, and a reputation that could get me killed at any time.

"But all that aside, I reckon I love you more than I ever thought it was possible to love anyone."

She walked up to me and said, "You've been going around feeling that way, and you haven't told me? I don't know whether to hit you or kiss you."

"If you're leaving the choice up to me," I said, "I'll take the kiss."

She smiled. My lips met hers and for a minute there I was as close to heaven as I ever figured to get. In my dream her lips tasted like wild honey, but I quickly learned that wasn't true. Wild honey never tasted that good.

The kiss ended far too soon and we walked back to the house hand in hand. I had, as my pa used to say, stepped in the trap with both feet. But I wasn't one bit sorry.

We sat and talked for hours. I turned in before dark, because I'd need some sleep for the big day ahead of me. At midnight I was up again, saddling Cap for the long ride to Alamitos. Mary Kay roused herself to see me off.

"Be careful," she said. "You get yourself shot up again and I'll never forgive you."

I kissed her softly. "You aren't about to get rid of me that easy," I said. "I'm afraid you're stuck with me for life."

"That's what I want," she said. "What worries me is how you keep trying to cut your life short."

I kissed her again, couldn't seem to get enough of that, and stepped up into the saddle. Pointing Cap into the darkness, I started for Alamitos.

CHAPTER 17

CAP and me came to Alamitos cross-country, keeping away from the main drags, and once in town I made my way to the jail by using the darkest alleys available. When I tied Cap behind the jail it was still an hour or so before first light.

I tapped on the back door, and after a minute it opened a crack, then all the way. Nolan was there, gun in hand. He holstered his Colt when he saw who it was and let me in. "You're just in time," he said. "It looks like everybody is here who's coming."

"How many did you get?"

"Twenty."

"*Twenty,*" I said. "I thought you'd have trouble finding half that many."

"So did I, but once folks knew what we wanted, why, it seemed they couldn't wait to volunteer. Come on up front and take a look."

We went on past the cells and into the front of the jail. That front office was a fairly large one, but it was jammed from wall to wall with men. Van Dorn, Juarez, and Schmidt were all there, and so was Harry Morgan. Harry had brought three of his own men along, and they looked plenty able to handle their end.

The only other men I knew were Doc Priter and Bill Flynn. We had a few minutes of getting to know each other, then got down to it. The first thing to do was transfer the office of county sheriff from Nolan to me. That proved to be fairly simple. Nolan handed Van Dorn a short, written resignation and gave me the badge. I pinned it on, and Van Dorn swore me in.

That done, Van Dorn gave Nolan a deputy's badge. Then he had every man in the room hold up his right hand and made deputies of them all. "Whatever happens today," he said, "we'll be on the right side of the law."

It was my turn to speak and I did it loud and clear, making certain every man in the room knew what his job was. The first thing I did was check with Van Dorn. "Did you get that ordinance passed?"

"It's on the books," he said, "and goes into effect at dawn today. The county sheriff, being you, now has the right to order anyone he deems undesirable to leave town or be jailed, providing they do not own property or have a permanent place of residence.

"Also, until further notice, no guns may be worn or carried north of the tracks except by duly authorized representatives of the law. That one will give us some trouble, I think. Folks want to be able to defend themselves."

"It's aimed at the gunhands and troublemakers," I said. "If some rancher or the like comes in wearing a gun, well, I won't worry about it. But a lot of towns are finding that guns and business don't mix well. It's about time Alamitos went in that direction, too."

Looking over the faces of the men, I spelled out my plan. There wasn't much to it. "What we are going to do," I said, "is clean out the town, and we're going to start with the Silver Slipper and the Bon Ton Hotel, then hit every saloon, whorehouse, and gambling hall.

"The rules are simple. Anyone wearing a gun who doesn't work for one of the trail drives coming, and most of the drovers will be out with the herds now, anyone like that is to be disarmed and brought to the jail.

"Harry can point out the crooked gamblers, and they go, too. If a man deals an honest game, let him alone. Anyone else, use your judgment. If you have any reason to believe he's a thief or troublemaker, haul him in and we'll sort it out after the fact."

Brigo Juarez cleared his throat. "I don't know," he said. "Out of twenty of us, not more than eight have used a pistol enough to have a chance against the kind of men we are going after."

"That's why we're going in groups," I said, "and it's why we're going so early. I want most of this job finished before they get the sleep from their eyes. As for being able to handle a gun, that isn't what we need.

"Nolan, start passing out the shotguns. If we do this right, we shouldn't have to fire a shot.

"One last thing," I said. "One of the men working for Ryan is named Dan Ames. We've reason to believe he might be at the Bon Ton, so I'll hit that first. But if he isn't there and one of you find him, make sure he doesn't slip away. We need him alive, but if you have to put a load of buckshot in his legs, don't hesitate.

"Now, try to relax. The saloons start opening their doors in thirty minutes and that's when we hit."

I sat down in the chair behind the desk and tried to take my own advice. Nolan kept himself busy making coffee . . . it took two full pots just to give each man a cup, but it was something to take his mind off what might be a tough day.

The sun topped the horizon and Alamitos began showing signs of life. Now was the time. I stood up and put my hat on. "Let's go," I said. "By breakfast I want the main street done."

We split into two groups, myself leading one and Nolan the other, and moved out of the jail. Speed was important now, but once we hit the Bon Ton and the Silver Slipper, things should ease more than a little. I stopped my group just outside the Bon Ton until Nolan was in position. Then we both moved.

Ten of us went through the door and into the lobby; ten men with grim looks on their faces and shotguns in their hands. The clerk behind the desk nearly had a heart attack. He stuttered a minute before finding his voice. "What's the meaning of this?" he said at last. "This is a hotel and our guests need their sleep."

, I walked up to the desk. "It's time all honest men were out of bed," I said. "Now give me the master keys."

"I can't do that. Mr. Ryan would have my skin."

I wasn't in the mood to argue. Reaching across the desk I grabbed a handful of shirt and jerked. He was a fair-sized man, but when I jerked he came half over the desk. My hand was closed tight up near his Adam's apple, and in a couple of seconds he was turning blue.

"You got a choice," I said. "You can worry about Ryan later, or you can worry about me now."

He gave me the keys. Passing them out, we climbed to the next floor and started down the hall, Van Dorn and four men taking one side and the rest of us the other. It worked like a charm. At least half the rooms were occupied by Ryan's men, but none of them wanted to tackle five shotguns at once.

As we found a man we pushed him down the hall ahead of us and went to the next room. In nine minutes we had nine men standing in the hall wearing only their long underwear. We herded them into a room, stationed a man outside and went on to the next floor.

We finished the second floor in about the same amount of time and were about to hit the top floor when we heard the shot. It was muffled, but obviously came from the floor above. We went up slowly, shotguns ready, but saw nothing.

The whole place was awake now, but we pulled men from the first several rooms without trouble. Then we came to a room where the door was already unlocked and cracked open about an inch. Thumbing back the hammer on my shotgun, I took a deep breath and kicked the door all the way open.

The room was empty except for the lone figure of a man slumped forward in a chair, blood from a head wound pooling at his feet. I knew who it was before I saw his face. The dead man was Dan Ames.

He'd been shot in the side of the head, the gun held so close that the powder flash had burned a large area of hair and skin. A .44-caliber derringer was wedged between the side of his leg and the chair.

"It looks like he killed himself," Van Dorn said. "Funny, he never seemed the kind who would do something like that."

"Killed himself, hell," I said. "Somebody pulled that trigger for him."

"Colby Ryan?"

"Ryan, or one of his killers. Either way it puts us back to square one. Ames was the best chance we had to put Ryan where he belongs."

I did a fair amount of cursing myself for a fool right then, but it didn't help. If I'd let Nolan take Ames in when he had the chance, Colby Ryan might be in jail now and the whole county at peace again.

I walked out of the room and looked down the hall. At the end of the hall was another room . . . one with a large, ornate door unlike any of the others. "That," Van Dorn said, "is Ryan's suite. Perhaps we should pay him a visit."

Walking to the door, I tried the master key. It didn't fit, and I was in no mood to knock. I kicked the door as hard as I could and the lock ripped free, sending splinters of wood everywhere as the door flew open.

Colby Ryan and Frank Heart sat at a small table, drinking coffee. Neither seemed surprised to see us. "Won't you join us?" Ryan said. "It's excellent coffee, and the way you boys have been working I'm sure you could use a cup."

"No thanks," I said. "I hate to stop work until the job is done. There's still a few men who need an escort out of town."

Ryan opened his eyes wide as if shocked. "Surely you don't mean me," he said. "After all, I am a respected business-man."

"You may be a lot of things, Ryan," I said, "but respected isn't one of them. No, you can stay . . . for a while." I looked at Frank Heart. "You, however, are another story."

"Frank works for me," Ryan said. "By what authority do you take it upon yourself to run gainfully employed men out of town?"

Van Dorn handed Ryan a copy of the new city ordinance. "This gives him the authority," he said. "Of course, you may challenge it in court, but that will take some time."

"And time," I said, "is something we have very little of. Get on your feet, Heart, and move out. Several of your friends are waiting for you. We wouldn't want them to get lonely."

He looked at Ryan. Ryan nodded and Heart stood up. "Someday, cowboy," he said, "I'm going to catch you without a gun."

I'd had enough of being threatened. I handed the shotgun to Van Dorn, turned, and backhanded Heart across the mouth all in the same move. Now, my hands are big and they're hard from wrestling mean cattle and meaner men. Heart's lip split like I'd used a knife, and blood spurted, drenching his shirt.

He staggered back, caught his balance, and charged, letting out a roar like a grizzly with a toothache. Frank Heart was a big man, outweighing me by at least thirty pounds, and he'd gone his whole life pushing smaller men around.

Thing was, most men knew next to nothing about fighting with their fists. When trouble came along they settled it with a gun or they let it go. Frank had done some fighting, but he always won through size and strength, knowing little more about technique than the average man.

That's where I had the advantage. I'd spent a lot of time working in a hard rock mine, and near six months helping put down railroad ties. A lot of Irish worked at both jobs, and most of those men were fighters. Several had fought in the ring, in fact, and by the time I left those jobs I knew how to use my fists.

When Frank Heart charged in, I just sidestepped a little and let him have one in the belly, then brought a left hook down on his jaw. The momentum of his charge, coupled with that left hook, slammed him to the floor hard enough to shake the whole room. He skidded along the carpet about three feet, giving himself a nasty burn on the face in the process.

But I'll say this for him, he didn't know the meaning of quit. With his lips and cheek bleeding and his face burned by the carpet, he got back to his feet and smiled. "You can hit pretty good," he said. "Now let's see if you can take a punch."

He moved toward me again, slower this time, his fists held high in front of his face. He jabbed a couple of times and I slipped them, then he caught me with a stiff right. That made me mad. He tried the same trick, jabbing quick and following it with a straight right.

I slipped the jab again, and when he threw the right I was waiting for it. He was coming at me and I stepped toward him, letting his right go over my shoulder and hooking my own right into his ribs at the same time. My fist landed and I felt ribs crack.

He howled in agony and clutched at his ribs. I hit him twice with my left and followed with a right that caught him square on the button. He went down in a heap.

Ryan sipped his coffee, not disturbed in the least. "You," he said, "can fight . . . a little. But when our time comes, I won't be that easy."

"Like I told you before," I said. "Anytime. Just anytime at all."

We walked back to the door, two of the men dragging Frank Heart behind them. At the door I stopped and looked back at Ryan. "By the way," I said. "Ames is lying in a room just down the hall with a bullet through his head. Don't suppose you'd know anything about that?"

"I thought I heard a shot," Ryan said. "Imagine that, Dan Ames killing himself. You just never know, do you?"

"Now why would you think he killed himself," I said. "I didn't mention anything about that."

Ryan jerked a little and spilled part of his coffee. His face turned hard. "One day," he said. "We are going to settle things. Just you and me. One day real soon."

I smiled and walked out. We herded all the men locked in the rooms out onto the street. Nolan and his men already had a fair-sized group waiting for us. "This is about all the jail will hold," he said. "We get many more and they'll be packed in like peas in a pod."

"I expect that's how we'll end up," I said. "I still want to sweep this town from one end to the other. We get too many guests we'll stack 'em in the office and post guards."

With the Silver Slipper and the Bon Ton out of the way, we started on the smaller hotels and saloons, plus several whore-houses and gambling halls. Once the town saw what we were up to it got to be a pitch-in affair. In an hour we had nearly a hundred honest citizens helping with the cleanup.

With that many men helping it went fast. In a bit over two hours we'd gone over Alamitos from one end to the other, and we'd hauled in more than fifty "undesirables." It was a far larger number than I'd anticipated, and most of them we stuck right in the middle of the street and put a ring of men around them, each with a double-barreled shotgun.

In spite of the size our operation grew to reach, there was very little trouble. One of our men was shot in the leg by a man who later proved to be wanted for a bank robbery. Not that it mattered. He fired one shot and three men near cut him in half with shotguns.

A few certainly slipped through the cracks or rode out of town before we got to them, but the obvious missing man was Con Ferris. He didn't turn up anywhere, and that bothered me. I'd no doubt he was still around, and even less doubt that one day I'd have to face him over the barrel of a Colt.

When we had all the gunmen, thugs, thieves, and sharps we thought we were going to get, or could handle, we started getting rid of them. That proved to be considerably more time consuming than gathering them in the first place.

I found wanted posters on more than a dozen of the men, but only five were for serious crimes. After sticking those five in a cell, we started dealing with the rest. We herded them all into the middle of the street and I mounted Cap so they could all see me.

"To make it simple," I said, speaking loud enough for all of them to hear, "we don't want you or your kind in Alamitos. You'll be given your horses, a few at a time, and you will ride out of town to the west.

"One thing, I don't give a damn where you go after you leave here, but if any one of you shows yourself in town again you won't be given a second chance."

"What about our guns," someone yelled, "and our personal gear?"

"You'll be given your clothing and the like after we've gone through it. As for your guns, you lost them."

With that we started the tedious process of going through their rooms and tracking down their horses from all the stables around town. It took most of the day, but by late afternoon the last of them had ridden out, and I was done in.

"We should have done this two years ago," Van Dorn said. "It would have saved a lot of trouble all the way around."

"Maybe," I said, "but sometimes you don't see things building until they get so big it's hard to handle them.

"Besides, this won't solve nearly as much of the trouble as you might think. It will give us a better chance to keep the peace inside of Alamitos, but outside of town nothing will change until Ryan is behind bars and most of the rustlers are put out of business.

"Thing we have to do now is not let the bad element build

back up. We can't keep them all out of town—we'd need a full-time army for that—but now we have the numbers under control. The best we can hope for is to keep it that way."

By the time the sun started slipping down behind the western horizon I was wishing I'd never laid eyes on Alamitos. Between the cowboys bringing in the herds, the prostitutes plying their trade, and the thugs, thieves, and drunks who'd slipped our net, Alamitos still had plenty of the wild life left.

I broke up two fights south of the tracks and hauled in a few drunks, and Nolan split a fellow's scalp who came at him with a knife, but all things considered, it wasn't too bad. But I was real close to being used up.

Time I threw my fourth drunk of the evening in a cell, all I wanted to do was ride back out to Zeb's, have supper with Mary Kay, and sleep for a week. I settled for greasy beef and beans from a boardinghouse not far from the jail and a few hours sleep on a cot in one of the cells.

CHAPTER 18

BY morning, however, I managed to get a decent amount of rest behind me and a good breakfast under my belt. I was ready to tackle one job that remained undone—tracking down all the cattle we thought were being held down around Horse Springs and hopefully breaking the backs of the rustlers in the process.

The time to do it was now, before Ryan could put together a plan to stop us. I started organizing a posse. With twenty men and ten days supply of food, we started south not long after noon. I dearly wanted to take Nolan along, but with both of us gone it would leave the town wide open, so I left him behind.

We swung by Zeb's ranch just so I could see Mary Kay for a few minutes. That made the whole trip worthwhile. I wanted to see John, but he'd gotten to feeling chipper and moved back to his own ranch, keeping the Coger brothers as hired hands.

We started south again, and for six days we pushed hard. Word had obviously reached the rustlers about the job we'd done cleaning out Alamitos, and when we caught up with them they were pushing the herd south for all it was worth.

You can only push cattle so fast, however, and we caught them. We had us a running gun battle for a few miles, then the rustlers, those still alive, figured no amount of cattle were worth dying for. When it was over we had four men in custody, three dead on their side and one on ours. Throw in two wounded on our side and one on theirs, none seriously, and that was it.

We also had better than two thousand head of rustled

cattle. Several hundred head of John's cattle were mixed in with cattle from nearly every ranch in the county. Funny thing though, out of all those cattle we didn't find a single steer owned by Colby Ryan.

We questioned the rustlers, but the story they told was just like I feared it would be. Jack Strayer or Dan Ames had always ridden out with orders, and while they were certain Ryan was giving those orders, none of them could make a connection that would stand up in court.

When you got right down to it, since Strayer and Ames were dead we couldn't even *prove* that they ever worked for Ryan. The fact that they were with him most of the time meant nothing. Unless I could find someone who had witnessed Ryan giving orders or breaking the law, he was going to remain free.

What we needed was a break, but waiting for something like that can make a man old and gray before the job gets done.

It would take two weeks or more to push all those cattle back up to where they belonged, and I couldn't afford to be away from Alamitos that long. I filled my saddlebags with food from the rustler's chuck wagon and started north, leaving the posse to deal with the cattle. I'd send riders from the ranches back to take over as soon as I could, but for now it was up to them.

When I reached Alamitos I was grimy with trail dirt and hadn't shaved in two weeks. I also smelled like I hadn't bathed in the same length of time. And I hadn't . . . unless you counted an accidental fall in a quick-moving river.

Nolan wasn't at the jail and I didn't go looking. First thing I did was buy enough clothes to give myself a change, then took a long bath at a barbershop and had the closest shave I could recall.

That barber threw in a haircut and a bottle of sweet-smelling hair tonic for free, and I left there feeling like a dandy. Nolan was back at the jail and did a double take when I walked in.

"Whoo-eee," he said. "You smell like a fancy Dan from one of those fun houses south of the tracks."

"Might do you good to get the same treatment," I said. "That girl of yours would likely fall head over heels."

"Might kick me head over heels, is more like it. She likes me just the way I am."

"No accounting for taste."

"That's all you know," he said. "Fact of the matter is, I done popped the question. We're getting hitched come a week from next Sunday."

"Well, that is good news," I said. "Though why a girl as pretty as that would want to marry a man with a badge on his chest is beyond me."

"I reckon you could put that question to Mary Kay," Nolan said. "I sure don't have the answer."

We spent some time talking and I filled Nolan in on the events with the rustlers. "You'd best send some riders around to the ranches and have them get some hands down there to take over the herd. Those men I left are going to be getting anxious about home cooking and seeing their women.

"Most of them aren't worth shucks at pushing cows anyway. We don't get some cowboys down there, they'll likely ride off and leave that herd to find its own way home."

"I'll get right on it," he said, "but there's something else that might interest you first. It's near lunchtime. Let's go grab a beer and a bite to eat. This may take some explaining."

We walked to a small restaurant about a block off the main street and took a table. It was a nice little place with red-and-white-checked tablecloths and curtains on the windows. A sign in front said Rosie's Home Cooking.

"I didn't think it was dignified for a deputy sheriff to be eating at some dive," he said. "Besides, Julie got herself a job here. Figured the least I could do was support her."

Julie picked that moment to come strolling from the

kitchen, and her face broke into a big smile when she saw Nolan. They greeted each other warmly, and her eyes never left his when we ordered our meal. When she walked off toward the kitchen I grinned at Nolan. "You found yourself a peach," I said. "You're a lucky man."

"Luckier than I can believe," he said. "But it sure sets a man to thinking. Running single, working for thirty a month and found suited me fine. With a wife and maybe kids to support, well, that puts another light on things."

That was pretty much the way I'd been thinking where Mary Kay was concerned. "You make almost twice that as deputy," I said. "For that matter, once we settle with Ryan, if we ever do, you can take back this badge, as far as I'm concerned."

"Seventy-five a month plus ten percent of the fines is good money," Nolan said. "You could raise a dozen kids with that kind of money."

"Maybe, if some drunk doesn't shoot me. No, I'll wear a badge for now, but it isn't for me either. Not in the long run."

Julie brought in our food and it looked mighty good, though it seemed Nolan's plate was piled a little higher than mine, and we were silent until our plates were scraped clean.

"You convinced me," I said. "Outside of Mary Kay's cooking, this is as good as any I've ever tasted. Reckon I'll do my eating right here from now on."

"Julie will be glad to hear that," he said. "Now, what I wanted to talk to you about. I don't know how much of what I'm going to tell you is true, but judge for yourself.

"Last night, I heard something real interesting. It seems someone broke into Ryan's office a couple of nights back. Ryan keeps a safe there, and he keeps a good deal of his money in that same safe. Whoever broke in knew the combination and cleaned it out. Can't say exactly how much was there, but the story goes it was over twenty thousand, and most of it in gold coin."

I whistled. "Even Ryan couldn't take that kind of a loss without hurting. I don't suppose anyone has filed a complaint?"

Nolan shook his head. "Might be the story ain't true, though I think it is. Might also be that Ryan doesn't trust us to bring the man in. It would be funny, him asking us for help, I mean."

"I can't see that happening," I said, "but he might just be afraid of what we'd find. Seems to me that Evan Cory said he was paid in gold coin. Not many are. It's too bulky to handle. But where does this take us, even if it's true?"

"I was just getting to that," Nolan said. "There's a little more to the story. Don't know how much it means, either, but some jasper got a look at the man who robbed the safe. Even put a name to the fellow. The name was Dave Burack."

That took my breath away. *"Dave Burack!"*

"That's right," Nolan said. "Now you tell me, what would Dave Burack be doing with the combination to Ryan's safe?"

Thoughts whirled around my head. Thinking never was my strong suit. "Might be somebody gave it to him for a share of the money. Or maybe he managed to open it without knowing the combination."

"Maybe," Nolan said. "But if that was the case, wouldn't Ryan be raising more of a fuss about losing all that money?

"The thing that makes me want to know more is this. Suppose, just for the sake of argument, that Burack was working a lot closer with Ryan than any of us knew."

I caught Nolan's train of thought. "Then he might know a lot of things that Ryan couldn't take a chance on us learning. If he complained to us about being robbed, and if we caught Burack, it might cook Ryan's goose."

"Exactly," Nolan said. "But this is still guess work. I can tell you this. I did some sign cutting out of curiosity, and somebody sure left town in a hurry. Whoever it was didn't use the road—he went northwest in a big hurry, right across country."

"How much of a head start would they have?"

"Likely two days anyway, and gaining more all the time. Still, a man who could track might catch him. By this time he probably believes he isn't being trailed."

I'd just got back into town and another long trail was the last thing in the world I wanted to see, but Nolan wasn't the kind of man who would bring something like this up unless he believed it would help us. Nolan was better on a trail than I was, but sending him out because I didn't want to do it didn't seem right.

We finished eating and walked back to the jail while I thought things over. As I started to open the door to the jail a long "Hellooo" filled the air. I turned to see Zeb and Mary Kay coming down the street in that old wagon of his. He stopped in front of the jail, and Mary Kay bounced to the ground and ran up to me.

I put my arms around her and hugged her soundly. "Why James," she said, "what are folks going to think with their sheriff acting this way right out in public?"

"They'll think he's in love," I said. "And they'd be right."

"In that case," Mary Kay said, "hug me again."

I did. She laughed. Then we went into my office, followed by Nolan and Zeb. Mary Kay sat down in the big green office chair behind my desk, and I sat on the edge of the desk, holding her hand.

"I didn't think you'd ever get back," she said. "And I ought to be mad at you. You didn't even stop and let me know you were back in town!"

"I'm sorry," I said. "I meant to, but you wouldn't have wanted to see me then anyway. Like as not you wouldn't have even recognized me for the dirt and beard."

"I suppose that's reason enough. The main thing is you're back again. I hated every minute you were away."

"So did I," I said, "but as much as I hate to, I have to start out again in the morning."

"Oh, no! How long will you be gone this time?"

"There's no way to tell," I said. "Maybe only a few days, maybe weeks."

I briefly went over what Nolan had told me about Ryan being robbed and about Burack. When I finished, Mary Kay squeezed my hand tighter. "I understand why you have to go," she said, "but I worry every minute you're gone. I keep seeing you lying along some lonesome trail, hurt or dying with no one to help."

"It goes with the job," I said. "Truth is, I feel safer out on the trail than I do here in town.

"I mean it. At least out there I pretty well know what I'm up against. In Alamitos, I never know who'll try to put a bullet in my back."

"At least we have this evening," she said. "I'd stay in town tonight if I could find a decent room."

"No need for that," Nolan said. "Julie found herself a nice little house right here in town. She has plenty of room and I know she wouldn't mind putting you up. She hasn't made too many friends in town yet and I'd take it as a favor myself."

"If you're sure she wouldn't mind," Mary Kay said.

Nolan put on his hat. "I know she won't," he said. "But I'll go clear it with her right now."

"You're just looking for an excuse to see her again," I said. "You aren't fooling anybody."

"Wasn't trying to. But seeing you and Mary Kay acting like lovebirds kind of made me want to go cut some didoes of my own. I'll be back in a few minutes . . . maybe."

Nolan went out and Zeb followed close behind. "Got shopping to do," Zeb said. "If I don't get away from all you love-struck young cows, I'll get lonely and start looking for my own filly."

"Just the thing for you," I said. "Nothing like a young filly to make a man feel good again. Add ten years to your life."

"Cut it short by ten years, is more likely," Zeb said. "But having a woman does have its fine points. Who knows, maybe

I'll look around a bit. Could be there's a widow or two just waiting for a man like me."

Zeb went on out and closed the door behind him. I pulled Mary Kay up out of the chair, sat down in it myself, then gave her a little tug. She dropped to my lap. She squirmed a minute to get comfortable and I like to died.

"If we don't get married real soon," I said, "I'm likely to make a real strong effort at turning you into a fallen woman."

"If we don't get married soon," she said, "I'm going to be tempted to let you."

"Nolan and Julie are getting married a week from Sunday," I said. "Maybe we ought to make it a double wedding?"

She threw her arms around my neck. "Nothing in the world would make me happier."

She kissed me, long and hard. When she let me up for air I smiled. "If I'd known you'd react like this," I said, "I'd have asked you a long time ago."

Nolan came back and told Mary Kay, "It's all set. And you're both invited to supper."

"We're all set too," I said. "When you get through with your wedding, we'll just keep the preacher there and let him get in another lick on us. If you don't mind sharing the stage, that is."

"Mind? If you hadn't brought it up, I was going to. I've faced down everything from grizzly bears to badmen, and never was really what you'd call scared. But just thinking about standing in front of a preacher has my knees shaking."

"I know what you mean," I said.

"Men!" Mary Kay huffed. "You ask us to marry you, expect up to spend the next forty years of our lives having your babies and mending your socks, then act like we tricked you into it. For two cents I'd join a convent and swear off men forever."

"It'll never happen," I said. "You love me too much."

I boosted her off my lap. "I've got to make my rounds and

earn my money," I said. "Why don't you run down to Rosie's and get aquainted with Julie?"

"Best be careful," Nolan said. "Get the two of them together after the way we've been talking and they'll likely be planning revenge."

"Now that," Mary Kay said, "is an idea."

Nolan showed Mary Kay the way to Rosie's while I went about the town, sticking my nose in first one place and then another, letting folks know I was about. I took my time, going to a few places that I might have passed by on a normal day, but the town was fairly quiet.

I dropped back in at the jail after my rounds and picked up Nolan, and we walked to Julie's house. It was a pretty, woodframe house, painted white with green trim, and the women were hard at work when we got there.

That was about as pleasant an evening as I could recall, just sitting about with good friends and talking, but all to soon it was time to turn in. I took Mary Kay out on the porch and said my good-byes there, while Nolan and Julie remained inside.

Nolan and me walked back to the jail together and stretched out on a couple of cots. Those cots were only thin blankets thrown over a set of springs, and while you might call them a lot of things, comfortable wasn't one of them.

I wanted to sleep, but thoughts were rushing around my head like leaves in a strong wind. Here I was about to get married and I had no idea at all of what I intended to do with my life. What I wanted was a ranch, but with a wife I'd have to find a place to live and a means of bringing home the bacon until we could get a place of our own.

And then, out of the blue, it came to me. I was going to take Mary Kay home.

My pa owned a fair-sized spread up Colorado way, and he'd been begging me to come up and help run it for some time. Pa still had a lot of years left in him, probably more than I did, in fact, but I could give him a helping hand and be able to put back a little money at the same time.

Mostly, I just wanted to see him again and get his advice. Me, I was more a doer than a thinker, but pa had it all over anybody I ever met when it came to using his head. Where I'd bow my neck and try to bull my way through a problem, pa'd give it a minute or two of hard thinking and come up with an answer.

Might be just the ticket for Nolan, too. He wasn't any keener on keeping a badge than I was, and one thing about a big ranch, you can always use another hand.

CHAPTER 19

I WAS up at first light, and getting off that cot was the best part of the whole night. It didn't take much to rouse Nolan, and we went out for breakfast. It was a chilly morning and I was stiff from spending the night on that cot, but what really made me cranky was the thought of riding off and leaving Mary Kay again.

Rosie's wasn't open yet, so we settled for ham and eggs at an all-night eatery that wasn't known for its home cooking. It didn't take much of that to fill me up, and we walked down to the livery, greasy eggs and rancid ham having made the day.

I packed a few supplies and we both saddled up, Nolan thinking to ride out with me far enough to show me where he cut the trail, but first we stopped in at Julie's. They had just gotten up themselves, but seeing Mary Kay made the day seem a whole lot brighter.

After drinking down two cups of good coffee with them, I made my good-bye and rode off with Nolan. He took me to the trail, still deep and distinct in the soft earth. I began following it, while Nolan headed back into town.

That morning got off to a shaky start, but there's something about being out on a trail alone that always perks me up, and this trail was a fine one. I was a northern boy as far as upbringing went. Once Pa bought that ranch in Colorado, we spent a few years there before I rode on, but it was Montana that I knew best.

Thing is, I'd always thought Montana country the prettiest anywhere, but it had nothing on New Mexico. Cap and me followed that trail off to the north, stayed with it as it turned a bit toward the east, and the country just seemed to rise up around us, getting higher and rougher and more beautiful with each mile.

Then I saw something that took the pleasure right out of me. Five riders had cut the same trail I was on, and danged if they hadn't turned to follow it. And from the stride of their horses, they wanted to end it quickly.

I pulled Cap up short and did some pondering. Burack's trail, if it was his, was a little more than two days old. The five riders now ahead of me had come along much more recently, but still had a good six hours or more on me.

It put me in a bad position. There was no way I could stay on the trail and reach Burack first, but to leave the trail would be a risk. I might lose it and not be able to pick it up again on down the line.

Nolan was the best tracker I ever knew, and I remembered something he once told me. Tracking, he said, is partly being able to read sign stamped in the ground, but the rest of it is being able to put yourself inside the head of the man you're tracking. Do that, and the game is more than half over.

All right. What would Burack do? What would I do in his place? One of three things. When you've a number of men on your trail, too many to fight with any hope of winning, you can head for rough country and try to lose them; you can try to outrun them and hope they quit; or you can head for a town and try to lose yourself in the crowd.

Which would Burack choose? Well, put yourself inside his head, I thought. What kind of man was he? He'd ridden some rough trails in his time, but of late he'd spent most of his days sitting behind the desk at the jail or drinking beer at the Slipper.

How much had that taken out of him? A man gets too used to being comfortable, and a long trail, especially one through rough country, can get tiring real fast. A few days of hard riding, staying in the saddle sixteen hours a day, can make any man wish for the comforts of town. Then, too, if

Burack had all that money from Ryan's safe, he might just be aching to spend it. After lying out somewhere in those mountains, his stomach growling and his back hurting from the hard ground, he'd get to thinking about all that money and what it could buy. He'd have thoughts of a soft bed and an easy woman, good food and all the whiskey he could drink.

He could get some pleasure in a small town, but to make full use of that money, and to be certain he could lose himself in the crowd, he'd need a town with some size to it. Going north as he was, that could be a problem.

There were a few towns up that way, but the biggest was just a flyspeck on the map, and most were so small they had to share the town drunk. But just a bit less than a hundred miles due north, over the line into Colorado, was a town that would fill the bill in every way.

Durango was a wide-open town, and losing yourself there with a pocket full of money would be easy . . . unless a man knew you were there and knew how to go about finding someone who didn't want to be found.

The trail was winding, following the Chaco River, and Burack was using all the skill he had to make trailing him difficult. He had a two-day or more head start, but he'd be losing a lot of time in keeping to the rough country. If I pushed hard, made a straight run for Durango, I might beat him there.

But if I guessed wrong about him going to Durango, I'd almost certainly lose Burack for good. On the other hand, if I stayed on the trail I'd not only be behind Burack, but those five other jaspers as well. And the way they were pushing their horses, I'd play hob catching up with Burack before they did. Catching him after wouldn't do much good.

I pointed Cap in the direction of Durango and took to riding. I wanted to find Burack, and I wanted to get back to Alamitos. There was a wedding taking place in about ten days that I wasn't about to miss for anything.

Cap had been pampered in his feeding ever since I owned him. I made sure he got plenty of corn in his diet because that gives a horse endurance—most outlaws wouldn't touch a horse fed only grass and hay . . . you get a posse on your trail and the last thing you want is the horse under you to give out.

I'd pushed Cap through hell a time or two and never once did he quit on me. He liked to run the way some men like to eat, me included, and once I let him know what I wanted he took to doing it. There were places where it was too rough to run, others where it was too steep. Now and again I gave Cap a chance to rest, but come nightfall we camped just short of the San Juan River.

I camped cold, making sure that Cap had good graze and plenty of water, and with first light we pushed on. We crossed over into Colorado and made Durango a bit after dark. Cap was about done in, so I left him at the first livery we came to, giving the old man there an extra dollar to see that Cap was well taken care of. Then I walked out to take a look at Durango.

It wasn't a cow town, but on first glance, the saloons seemed filled with the same wild-eyed cowboys who flocked to Alamitos. Closer examination revealed another story.

While most of the men were dressed somewhat similar to the average cowpoke, most of them wore work boots rather than riding boots and only a few had the lean build of a man who spent his life in the saddle. Fact is, most of the men were miners, and others were drifters and general riffraff.

If Burack was coming to town he would likely be there already, and I went to looking. First thing I did was take off my badge and slip it out of sight. My jurisdiction ended back at the Colorado line and the local law might frown on my being there.

Starting in the higher-class saloons, I struck up a conversation here and there, friendly like, and after a while mentioned that I was looking for a friend of mine. Then I described Burack and tossed in that he was a free spender and a man who liked easy living and easier women.

It wasn't long before I had a line on someone who filled the bill. A man had ridden in the night before and had gone from saloon to saloon, throwing around double-eagles like they were so much lead. It took another two hours to track him to a high-class whorehouse a good bit off the beaten track. I walked on down to it, took one look at the place, and hoped Burack had taken as much money as rumor said.

The whorehouse didn't have a sign or anything like that, but there was no mistaking it. It was a big, rambling, two-story building set on a hill that was just outside the city itself. A pair of red lanterns flooded the front of the house with garish light, and the place was lavishly decorated. This would be where the big shots and the free spenders came to find a good time.

I walked to the place and started up the steps to the porch that spanned the front of the house. Two burly men stood near the door, and they didn't look at all friendly. As I neared the door one of them stepped in front of me and shoved a beefy hand against my chest. "You better turn around and go back down the hill," he said. "This place isn't for the likes of you."

"I thought it was for anyone with enough money in his pocket," I said. "What else does it take?"

"More than you've got," he said.

Well, I had money, but what I didn't have was patience. The man with his hand against my chest blinked, and when he opened his eyes that Colt of mine was threatening to push his nose out the back of his head. Funny how a thing like that will make a man easy to get along with.

"Mister," I said, "I'm tired, hungry, and short on time. All I want to do is go through that door and talk to the madam running this show.

"Now, we can do this one of two ways. You can step aside

and let me pass, or I could pull this trigger and see if your friend is more agreeable."

He didn't like it, but you never saw a man back away from a door so fast in your life. Slipping my Colt back in the leather, I turned the doorknob.

The door opened into kind of a greeting room, and I never saw so much silk and fancy doodads. The carpet was thick and obviously new, and some of the paintings on the walls would have made a sailor blush.

A door opened to my right and a blonde woman a shade over forty came out, her smile slimming down when she saw me. She was wearing a corset and an open, silk robe, and through the open door behind her I could see half a dozen or more younger women.

The blond woman mustered her smile again and walked right up to me. "You could do with a bath," she said, "but if you have the money we can handle that . . . along with someone to scrub your back."

"Thank you, ma'am. I'm sorry about the way I look, but I just got in off the trail. Fact is, I'm just looking for a friend."

"Call me Maggie," she said. "You pick out the friend you want and we'll talk price."

That flustered me some, and it was starting to be an effort to keep my thoughts straight. "No, ma'am," I said quickly. "I mean, thanks, but I really am looking for a friend. A fellow."

Maggie sighed. "That's too bad. What makes you think he's here?"

"Old Dave," I said, "likes nothing better than to have a good time, and after seeing you, ma'am, I'd say if a man couldn't have a good time here, he just wasn't trying."

"Dave, huh? Can you describe him?"

I gave her his description. "Dave Burack is his right name, ma'am . . . free-spending Dave we call him. He has plenty of money and doesn't mind throwing it around. Never knew a man who thought more of having fun."

"He's here, all right," she said. "Been here since late last night. You sure described him right, too. He's gone through half the girls already, and no sign of slowing down."

She turned around and yelled through the open door behind her. "Rhonda, come on out here a minute."

A red-haired woman came out of the room, and my breath went out with a whoosh. She wasn't more than twenty, pretty as anything.

"This fellow is here," Maggie said, "to find someone. Would you take him up to Debbie's room?"

"Be glad to," Rhonda said. "Just follow me."

She started up the stairs and I went along behind her. We reached the second floor and she stopped, pointing down the hallway. "My room is just down there," she said. "Are you sure you wouldn't like to make a little detour? Your friend will wait."

I had to think real hard about Mary Kay right then. I cleared my throat. "Ma'am," I said. "I'm to be married in a little over a week. I guess I better just go ahead and find Dave."

She puckered her lips. "Some of my best customers are married," she said, "but I guess it can wait."

She took me to a door about twenty feet down the hall. "This is Debbie's room," she said. She started to knock and I caught her hand. "I'll take it from here," I said. "You run on back downstairs."

She walked away and I watched her until she was out of sight. When she was gone I just opened the door and stepped inside. Half the room was filled with the biggest bed I ever saw, and Dave Burack was stretched out on his back in the middle of the bed, buck naked and in the act.

When I opened the door he looked up, but there just wasn't anything he could do.

"Hello, Dave," I said. "Fancy meeting you here."

Dave dropped back and closed his eyes. The woman lay there looking at me, trying to understand whether to be mad or scared. "You'd best get dressed," I said. "Both of you."

The woman got up and slipped on a robe, and Dave moved to get his own clothes. "Not yet," I said. I checked his clothing, going through each piece and then tossing it to him. I came up with a Colt .45 and the neatest little hideaway gun you ever saw. I laid the guns on the dresser and waited for Burack to pull his clothes on.

When he was dressed he pulled a wallet from his jacket. "Do you mind if I pay her," he said, "or do you intend to keep all the money for evidence?"

"She earned it," I said.

I couldn't tell how much Burack gave her, but it was enough to make her eyes light up. She left the room and Burack looked at me. "I figured Ryan would try to follow me," he said, "but I never counted on you. What now?"

"That's up to you," I said. "Talk to me and we might work things out."

Hope showed on his face. "I'll tell you anything you want to know."

"You know what I want. I want something that can put Ryan where he belongs. You give me that and we can work something out."

He took a cigar from a fancy case and lit it, then extended the case toward me. "Cost a dollar each," he said.

I took one and lit it. It was worth a dollar. "We don't have a lot of time," I said. "In case you didn't know, there's at least five men on the trail besides me."

"I do know, but I gave them the slip." He puffed on the cigar and thought a minute. "Why not," he said at last. "What have I got to lose?

"You won't believe it, but a few years ago I was more like you than you'd believe. Never did a dishonest thing in my life, worked behind the badge, and believed in what I did. Then I fell in with Colby Ryan. Easy money got the better of me. Maybe putting Ryan away will make up for some of the things I done."

"It'll help," I said. "It'll help a lot. You come back and

testify against Ryan and you'll be able to walk away with your head up."

Burack slowly shook his head. "I'd never live to see the courtroom. Besides, you don't need me to testify. The answer has been there all the time. All you got to do is get a court order to examine the books at the bank.

"Chet Watkins and Colby Ryan have been in bed together since Ryan came to Alamitos. Watkins has two sets of books. You want the set he keeps in a safe behind a bookcase in his office.

"If you need something else you got to go out to Ryan's ranch. About two miles due east of his ranch house you'll find a boulder. It's reddish brown and big as a house—you can't miss it. Anyway, dig about forty yards straight south from that boulder and you'll find two of the ranchers who came up missing."

"Ryan buried them on his own land?"

"Why not? What else would you do with bodies you didn't want found? Throw 'em in a river and they float, bury them on somebody else's land and some farmer or prospector might dig them up accidentally.

"Nobody goes on Ryan's land but Ryan's men. I guess I'm about the only man left alive except for Ryan who knows where those bodies are.

"You check those books and dig up those bodies," he said, "and you can hang Colby Ryan."

Me, I kind of leaned back and looked at him. The whole thing might have been a wild yarn he was spinning just to get himself off the hook, but it had the ring of truth about it. And tying Chester Watkins to Colby Ryan cleared up some questions.

I'd always wondered how Ryan got the money he needed to build so fast. Even with the robberies and rustling there was a hole to fill. When Ryan first came to Alamitos there wasn't much money in the area to steal, and the ranches were just starting to build.

"All right," I said. "I'll check it out. But if I find you've lied to me . . ."

"It's the truth. What happens to me now?"

"That's up to you," I said. "As far as I'm concerned you have a free ticket."

"What about the money?"

"I figure that money belonged to Evan Cory, and he had no next of kin. You may as well keep it. But if I was you, I wouldn't stay around here too long. It might be a great way to spend money, but if I could find you, so could Ryan."

I walked out and went down the stairs. A customer had come in and Rhonda was leaning against the doorway, looking him over. As I went out the door she called to me, "Come back real soon. And be sure to ask for me."

I tipped my hat and went out. Those two guards were still there, but they paid me no mind as I walked away.

Walking slowly back the way I came, I got maybe a hundred yards from there when a clatter of hooves made me look back. A group of riders, five I counted, were dismounting in front of the whorehouse. Two of them led their horses around behind the house, another stayed out in front, and the last two walked up onto the porch.

It was too dark and too far to make out a face, but something about the way one of the men moved as he stepped to the porch made my heart jump. I could be wrong, but I'd have bet my left foot that it was Colby Ryan.

Breaking into a run, I went back at full speed. That fellow who stayed out front with the horses saw me coming, but too late. He tried to pull his gun, but mine was already out and I laid the barrel right across his face. He went down like he'd been shot, and I kept right on going. Those two on the porch knew enough to get out of my way, and I hit the door with my shoulder at top speed.

It crashed open and I saw Maggie sitting in the corner, an ugly bruise already forming on her cheek. Before she could speak a pistol shot roared from somewhere upstairs, followed quickly by two more. I went up the stairs, three at a time.

A man with a pistol appeared at the top of the stairs. Throwing myself sideways, I fired twice, my bullets crossing his. Something tugged at my shirt, but he wasn't so lucky. Clutching at his chest he fell forward, nearly taking me with him as he tumbled down the long stairway.

Looking down the hall, I saw that the door to Burack's room was open. At that moment Colby Ryan stepped into view. We fired at the same time, his bullet hissing past my ear and my own striking the doorjamb near him.

I jumped around a corner and tried to catch my breath. I ejected the empties from my Colt, shoved three fresh rounds into the cylinder, then peeked around the corner. A flash of red came from down the hall and a bullet struck the wall within inches of my face, spraying me with slivers of wood.

I jerked back and wiped at my eyes. Trying again, I went low, stuck my Colt around the corner, and fired twice. Ryan let out a yelp and jumped away from the door. A moment later I heard the sound of breaking glass. Taking a chance, I started down the hall toward Burack's room, going slow, Colt extended out in front.

I went through the door hard and fast, ready to shoot. There was nothing to shoot at. Dave Burack lay on the floor, clutching his shoulder and moaning, but Ryan hadn't waited around. The window was smashed and he was gone.

I ran to the window and looked out. It opened onto a section of the roof that sloped gently downward. A rifle roared in the night and glass broke above my head. I emptied my pistol at the flash and ducked back to reload.

The sound of running horses came to my ears, and suddenly the room was filled with men, one of them wearing a badge. He had a long-barreled Remington in his hand and an unhappy look on his face.

It took some fast talking, but after a few minutes we had things straightened out, Maggie and Rhonda both putting in a good word for me. A deputy came in several minutes later and slowly shook his head. "It's a mess," he said. "Got one fellow out front with half his teeth missing, a dead man at the bottom of the stairs, and a gut-shot one out back."

A doctor came in and took a quick look at Burack's shoulder. "I've hurt myself worse than this shaving," he said. "You'll be fine in a couple of days. That'll be ten dollars."

The marshal looked at me and rubbed his face with a beefy hand. "I guess your story checks out all right," he said. "You planning on being in town long?"

"Planned to leave at first light," I said.

"That's good. Real good. You got to understand, son, I ain't unfriendly, but I already got more trouble than I can handle."

The marshal went on back to his duties and the room slowly cleared. Burack was on the bed.

"Did Ryan get the money?" I asked.

He shook his head a little. "Most of it isn't even here," Burack said. "And you didn't give him time to pry the whereabouts of it out of me. He's running back to Alamitos as broke as when he left."

"Broke? I can see where losing that money would hurt him, but he must be worth a hundred thousand or more."

"Not really. He doesn't own all that much land, and a lot of what he does own he can't sell. The deeds wouldn't stand up. Sure, he has plenty of cattle and the Slipper. He owes more on the Bon Ton than it's worth. He could raise plenty of cash to get by on, if given a little time, but you won't give him that, will you?"

I walked to the door, stopped, and looked back. "No," I said. "With what you've told me, I think Ryan is about out of time. Are you going to be all right?"

Burack smiled. "You funnin' me? I got a whole carpetbag full of money and the best whorehouse you ever saw to

recuperate in. Reckon I'll just stay here till my shoulder heals
. . . or my money runs out."

I found a cheap hotel room in town. Come first light I
rode out of Durango, pointing Cap back the way we came.

CHAPTER 20

CAP had been pushed hard on the way to Durango and I eased up a bit on the return trip. But Cap was a sight better horse than Ryan would have, and I thought there was an outside chance I could catch him before we reached Alamitos. It proved not to be so easy.

Ryan had a man with him, and before that trail was two hours old I saw that Ryan was taking no chances. I found Ryan's companion face down on the trail, the back of his head blasted away by a bullet. Ryan now had two horses and could switch back and forth.

I thought of buying a horse somewhere to keep up, but unless I got lucky it would take a detour of some kind to find one. So Cap and I stayed well behind Ryan all the way to Alamitos.

It was about breakfast time when I got to Alamitos, and I found Nolan at Julie's. Me, I was about done in. What I wanted to do was sleep, but Ryan came first. Actually, putting away half the food in Julie's kitchen came first, but then I turned my thoughts to Ryan.

I explained to Nolan all that had happened in Durango and asked about Colby Ryan. "He rode in just before dark last night," Nolan said. "I could tell he'd been on a long, hard trail, but there was no reason to tackle him."

"There is now," I said. "Let's go pay a call on him."

We walked down to the main street and started toward the Bon Ton. Nolan pointed down the street toward the bank. "What do you reckon is going on down there," he said. "Looks like a pretty good crowd forming."

The idea popped in our heads at the same time and we

174

sprinted to the bank. Shoving through a dozen men, we reached the front door. "Don't understand it," somebody said. "Chet always has the door open long before now. Must be sick or something."

"If he was sick," I said, "one of his clerks would have opened it."

"I am one of his clerks," the man said. "He doesn't trust us with a key."

Figured. Could be a lot of reasons for the bank not yet being open, but I was in no mood to go searching the town for Watkins. Making everyone stand away from the door, I kicked it open. Chet Watkins was on the floor behind the counter, his blood splattered on the wall beyond him.

The door to the safe stood wide open and there wasn't so much as a worn dollar bill left inside. "You'd better round up a posse," I told Nolan. "Have them ready to go in half an hour."

While Nolan went to handle that, I went to take care of a horse. Cap was used up and would need several days of rest and food before he'd be ready for another trail. I was in about the same shape, and Colby Ryan was probably near the end of his own string. But while Cap could rest, I had to keep pushing a while longer.

I picked a horse that looked good, saddled him, and went to see how Nolan was coming with the posse. You never saw so many men volunteering to do something. Seemed most of the folks in town and a lot of folks from other places had money in the bank, and they all wanted it back.

The cattle buyers and some of the herd owners were raising the biggest fuss, and they had plenty of cowboys willing to ride after Ryan. We could have deputized several hundred men if we'd taken the notion, but we settled for an even dozen, Nolan and myself included.

We picked up Ryan's trail and started along it. Before long I was getting worried. The trail skirted right along the eastern edge of the Malpais Lava Flow, and if Ryan kept to it, he'd cut right across Zeb's ranch. I kicked that horse of mine in the belly and he jumped ahead like he knew what I was afraid of.

The trail continued to aim for Zeb's ranch, right for the heart of it, and by the time Zeb's house came into sight, my heart was pounding. The trail led right to Zeb's door and I was off my horse and through the house without much more than slowing down. Zeb was tied and gagged in a back room. Mary Kay was gone.

Zeb was throwing a fit to get loose, and I quickly took off his gag and untied him. "He took Mary Kay," Zeb gasped. "The bastard took Mary Kay."

Most of the other men had followed me in the house and we formed a circle around Zeb as he told his story. "Came bursting in with no warning at all," Zeb said. "Caught me napping. Mary Kay put up a fight, but Ryan was too strong for her. Too strong for me too."

"There was nothing you could do," I said. "Don't worry, Zeb. We'll get Mary Kay back."

"You can't," he said, "not all of you. Ryan said he'd kill her if he saw anybody but you on his trail, and he meant it. He wants you to follow him, but anybody else will get her killed."

I stood straight up and swore. "There it is," I said. "I'm going on alone. There isn't any other choice."

"What about the money?" one of the men asked. "We can't let him get away with the town's money."

"I'm going alone and that's it!"

A couple of the men started to argue, but Nolan cut them short. "You heard the man," he said. "Any one of you tries to follow him and I'll lay your skulls open with the barrel of my pistol."

Nolan meant it and the rest of those men never said another word. I didn't wait for yes or no, but ran outside and started down that trail. I hadn't been on it for more than a couple of hours when Ryan pulled a fast one. He swung to the east, then circled until he was riding north, straight for Alamitos.

That threw me. If he rode anywhere close to that town he would find himself dancing at the end of a rope. But before long I was riding along the lava flow again, this time on the east side. Ryan had ridden down one side of the Malpais and was now riding back up the other.

Then, with the rough red walls of the lava flow towering to my left and a lot of wide open country to my right, his trail simply disappeared. The ground was sandy and loose, but the print of his horse was plain . . . until it simply wasn't there. It was like that horse had taken to flying. It disappeared just that quick.

Right there I sure could have used Nolan, but I had to reply on my own knowledge of how to find a lost trail.

Ryan hadn't backtracked, and he hadn't gone east, and there was no way he could hide a trail in that ground. That meant he went straight ahead. He must have brushed away his trail, likely using one of his blankets.

Getting off my horse, I examined the ground closely. Sure enough, there were brush marks in the sand. Another couple of hours and the wind would have blown away all trace of the trail, but I was close enough behind him to see them. Trouble was, those brush marks led me right to a blank wall of the lava flow. Study got me nowhere. The trail led right to a blank wall.

The lava wall sloped very gently for fifteen feet, humped a little, then went straight up. A horse could scramble up that slope easy enough, but after that was a wall that a mountain goat couldn't climb.

But I found fresh marks on the slope that might have been made by a horseshoe. My head spinning, I walked up the slope, leading my horse. When I reached the top, I got the shock of my life.

There was a space about ten feet wide between the back of that slope and the rock wall, and a trail ran through a crack and vanished into the depths of the lava flow. I mounted my horse and followed the trail, going slow and careful.

After a hundred yards I got to an enclosed area of green. The lava had flowed around some high ground and left better than forty acres of land open to the sky. The grass was knee-deep and from somewhere I caught the sound of running water. And off to my left, built right against the wall, stood a small cabin.

Tied in front of the cabin was a pair of horses. One of them was Mary Kay's.

Ryan must have been watching for me, because no sooner had I spotted the cabin than the door opened and Ryan came out. He was holding Mary Kay in front of him, his arm around her throat. In his other hand he held a pistol.

"Ride over here," he shouted. "And don't try anything."

Doing as he told me, I pulled up short about twenty feet in front of him. "Get down off that horse, slow," he said, "and take off your gunbelt."

I did it, having no choice while he shielded himself with Mary Kay. He made me toss the gunbelt away, then ordered me to start backing away. When I was safely away from my horse and guns he told me to stop, then shoved Mary Kay back toward the door of the cabin. "You can watch through the window," he told her. "But if you stick your pretty nose outside I'll break it."

"Do like he tells you," I told her. "Everything will be fine."

She didn't like it, but she went inside. Ryan looked at me and smiled. "I've dreamed of the day when I'd have you in this position," he said. "Without your gun you're just another cowboy."

"What now?" I asked. "Going to put a bullet in me? It won't help. You'll never get away."

His eyes flashed. "Putting a bullet in you is exactly what I should do, but that would be too quick and easy. I want you to suffer a long time before you die.

"As for getting away, I already have. Once you're dead I'll

brush away your tracks, and this time I'll do it right. You found me because I wanted you to.

"I have a month's supply of food in that cabin. By then they'll have stopped looking. Then I'll ride down to Lincoln County. That whole county is ripe for picking, and I have the money to pick it."

He walked right up to me. With one move he tossed his Colt away and swung a wicked left that caught me high on the cheek and sent me sprawling. He held up his fists and laughed. "I told you once that somebody would beat you down to size," he said. "I've killed a man with my fists, and I could have killed others. Now I'm going to kill you, but first I want you to know what pain really is."

My ears were still ringing from the blow, but I climbed to my feet and circled warily, my weight on the balls of my feet for balance. I threw a quick jab that caught him in the mouth, but did no real damage.

Ryan was bigger and nearly as quick. On strength we were about even, but in spite of all the fighting I'd done, he obviously had more experience by far. He stepped in suddenly, feinted with a left, then caught me with a solid right that shook me all the way to my heels.

I staggered, but stayed on my feet. We traded a couple of jabs, then I hit him in the belly with a right hook that had all my weight behind it. It was like hitting a tree trunk. Ryan threw a short uppercut that buckled my knees, and I barely slipped the following right that would have put me away for good.

As I slipped the punch, Ryan backheeled me and I went down. Without hesitating, he swung a big boot at my head. I jerked my head to one side out of pure instinct. The boot missed, but his spur raked across my cheek, splitting it wide open and barely missing my eye.

Rolling quickly away, I came to my feet and wiped blood from my face. I was breathing hard and I was scared. Truth was, after all I'd gone through, I simply wasn't in shape for a long fight. If I was to have any chance at all, it would have to be soon.

But Ryan was good. Very good. Big, fast, strong, and experienced, Ryan was every bit the fighter he claimed to be. For two solid minutes we stood toe to toe, trading punches, both of us landing, but Ryan getting the better of it.

He split my lip with a straight left, then did the same thing to my ear with a right cross, and it hurt like hell. But it was that right cross that gave me a chance.

He'd been throwing it from the start with devastating results. Only luck had saved me so far, but at last I noticed that just before he threw that right he always dropped his shoulder a couple of inches.

Backing away as he came in, I worried at him with left jabs and waited. When his right shoulder dropped again I stepped to the left and threw a hook that crossed his right. It caught him right on the button and stopped him in his tracks. I followed with three right to the belly, throwing them from the hip and getting my legs behind the punches.

He shoved me away, but for the first time I saw worry on his face. Those punches had hurt him and put doubt in his mind. He came at me, slower, caught me with a left, and threw that right cross again.

It worked again, and this time when I threw that left hook it caught him coming in. I felt the shock of the punch all the way to my shoulder. Ryan froze in his tracks, a dazed expression on his face. I hit him twice more with the left and followed with a right that started somewhere in southern Texas and gathered speed all the way.

That punch caught Ryan on the point of the chin and he went down . . . and started to get up. Me, I couldn't believe it. If he'd hit me like that I'd have been out for an hour. I was done in, bloody, weak, and gasping for every breath. If Ryan got back to his feet I was dead.

Grabbing a handful of his hair as he reached his knees, I hit him four times with everything I had left, then brought my knee up and caught him square on the nose. It exploded like a ripe tomato and Ryan went down.

I stood there and looked at him for a moment, hands on knees and gasping for breath, then turned and started slowly for the cabin. I hadn't made more than twenty feet when Mary Kay burst from the door. "Look out," she screamed. "He's got a gun!"

I spun toward Ryan and saw him standing twenty feet away, his face a mask of blood. Somehow he'd managed to reach the Colt he had tossed away before the fight, and now was fumbling with it, his hands bruised and swollen from the fight. My own gun was too far away, but I still had my sheath knife.

My own hands were in bad shape, and it took a couple of tries to wrap my fingers around the hilt of the knife. Then I found my grip, pulled the knife, and threw it just as Ryan fired. His bullet spat dirt from between my feet. My aim was a little better.

The center of his body was my target, but the knife sailed high, taking Ryan in the throat and going in to the hilt. He dropped the Colt and grabbed at the knife, making horrible gagging noises as he tried to pull it free.

He fell face down, kicked a couple of times, and died.

Then, not caring about the blood or anything else, Mary Kay was in my arms. I held her tight and nothing in my whole life had ever felt half as good.

After a spell, Mary Kay made an effort to treat my cuts and managed to stop the bleeding. I retrieved my knife and the money Ryan had stolen, then we started for Alamitos.

CHAPTER 21

WHEN Sunday rolled around I was still bruised and sore, the cuts healing, but not pretty to look at. Mary Kay wouldn't have any part of putting off the wedding for a couple of weeks though, and I figured if she could stand to look at me, then everyone else could, too.

With the girls already down to the church, Nolan and me used Julie's house to spruce ourselves up. The way my face was banged up that was quite a chore, but I climbed into a fancy suit and did my best.

I reckon most folks would have counted Nolan and me as brave men, but you never saw two more wobbly-kneed, pale-faced, nervous examples of manhood in your life than we were right then. Finally Nolan swallowed hard and looked at me. "I guess we best get on down there," he said, "and face the music."

Sounded for all the world like a man about to face his own hanging. "Yeah," I said. "I guess so."

I strapped on my Colt over that fancy suit and Nolan looked at me funny. "I'll take it off once we reach the church," I said, "but I paid near twenty dollars for these duds, and I don't aim to have some jasper fill them full of bullet holes until I've had my use of it."

We went out and started down the street. Turning a couple of corners we came in sight of the church. My knees got weaker with every step, and my mouth got drier. But I kept walking, keeping my mind firmly on *after* the wedding rather than the ceremony itself.

Only a few yards from the steps leading up to the church, the stillness and my own thoughts were shattered by a ringing voice coming from directly behind me. Something seemed to sink in the pit of my stomach, and I turned slowly, knowing what I would see.

Con Ferris was standing in the middle of the street thirty yards away, his feet spread wide. "Darnell," he shouted. "Turn around. It's time."

Ferris was the one loose end, and while he'd always been in the back of my mind, I'd hoped that it was over. He'd slipped through our net, causing me to hope that he had ridden away, and once Ryan was dead . . . well, whatever I thought, I was wrong.

I looked at the ground for a second or two, a feeling of depression strong within me. Seemed the killing was never going to end, and I was tired of it. But there was nothing for it now. It was kill or be killed and that left little choice.

My hand was still sore from the fight with Ryan, and I didn't know how fast I could draw a gun. Ferris stood there, calm and confident, waiting for me. Flipping the tail of my jacket out of the way, I started toward him. When I was within twenty yards he pointed a finger at me. "That's close enough," he said. "Stop right there."

I kept walking, measuring my steps, never taking my eyes off Ferris. Each step took me a yard closer. At ten yards Ferris backed off a step. "*Stop*," he said. "Stop right there or I'll draw."

I was taking a gamble and well I knew it, but it was a thing I'd noticed with most men, and it held true with Ferris. The thing was this: when you're fast and good, you know that a man standing a little distance away is at a big disadvantage unless he's at least as fast and good as you are.

But up close, up real close, up where you're nose to nose and eye to eye, good doesn't mean as much. At that range you can't miss, and the chances are about even that both men will take a bullet.

Ferris knew that as well, and he wasn't going to let it happen. I took two more steps and he drew, his hand flashing down faster than my eye could follow, but in his haste to kill me before I got to close, he fired a split second too quick.

His bullet tore through my now empty holster, and my own, fired just after his, slammed him in the chest. He staggered, a red stain spreading rapidly across his shirt. He tried to bring his Colt back in line, but I stepped to the right, making him shift his aim, and I fired twice more, both shots hitting home.

The Colt fell from his hand, but he raised his arm anyway, seemingly unaware that his hand was empty. Then he fell to the ground, and I saw the life go out of him.

Turning back to the church, I found most of the people had come outside at the sound of the shots. All I focused on was Mary Kay, looking lovelier than I'd ever imagined a woman could look. She wore a wedding dress that was meant only for her, designed for an angel.

I walked to her and took her hand in mine. "Let's get married," I said. "It's all over at last."

We went inside, and you know, I made it all the way through the vows without missing a word.

If you have enjoyed this book and would like to receive details on other Walker Western titles, please write to:

Western Editor
Walker and Company
720 Fifth Avenue
New York, NY 10019